Also by this author -

**"And So Forth And So On,
Memoirs of an Ordinary Man"**

Terra Incognita
And Other Stories

Andrew Frank Klimko

authorHOUSE®

AuthorHouse™
1663 Liberty Drive, Suite 200
Bloomington, IN 47403
www.authorhouse.com
Phone: 1-800-839-8640

First published by AuthorHouse 1/21/2008

ISBN: 978-1-4343-3436-7 (e)
ISBN: 978-1-4343-3437-4 (sc)

Library of Congress Control Number: 2007906542

Printed in the United States of America
Bloomington, Indiana

This book is printed on acid-free paper.

Our firmest convictions are apt to be the most suspect, they mark our limitations and bounds. Life is a petty thing unless it is moved by the indomitable urge to extend its boundaries.

- Jose Ortega y Gassett

For those who taught us when we did not wish to learn and for those who found an indomitable urge to learn.

CONTENTS

Affinity

I HAVE TO WRITE this now. Before it is forgotten. Forgetting is something we all do quite easily. We forget our past. And are we truly aware of our present? Is it not clear that we seldom wonder who we are, or why we are here. Is that not so? We become absorbed in the world around us to such a degree that we live almost zombie-like, functioning almost automatically. In short we become unaware of our life, lost in our likes and dislikes, avoiding pain and seeking pleasure. We live by habits, not attempting to understand existence but instead reacting to the multitude of jumbled thoughts robbing us of our attention. Do we possess them or do they possess us?

Yet there is an inner world. There must be. That is what I need to write about. At first I gave little thought to such a concept, ignoring it if it dared to surface in my consciousness. With a good deal of ambivalence the idea oscillated, flitting about in my mind until I grew aware of it and its compelling nature. Because I had been teaching history and philosophy I believed that I was different and that I was immune to what others faced. That's the curse of the intellect when bowing to the pressure of the ego. Then my understanding of the inner world came into sharp focus after meeting an unusual stranger. It happened one day as I sat on a park bench reading a newspaper, trying to lose myself in the problems of others instead of confronting those of my own. The strange sensation of being watched caused me to look around. There was nothing exceptional within sight, just a tired looking old man sitting on another bench nearby. My gaze returned to my newspaper. Someone nearby coughed. It was him, the old man. He turned and looked at me intently for a moment. His glance in my direction somehow seemed unsettling.

This meeting occurred on a balmy summer afternoon. There was a pleasant breeze that along with the shade of the large trees worked to nullify the heat of the sun. The trees formed a canopy and occasionally the slight wind moved through the leaves parting branches allowing the sun's rays to flash across his face before it slipped away into cool dark shadows. The flickering light captured and accentuated a placid countenance.

I grew fascinated by him and began staring at him for unexplained reasons wondering who he might be. He may have been a professional of some kind, an accountant or a lawyer, or perhaps a doctor. He wore a suit and although he appeared formal he did not seem standoffish or pompous. Others might have been intimidated by his unique presence. Maybe he was a priest or a stage actor. He could have been many things. At one point he pulled out a large pocket watch and glanced at it before shoving it back into a vest pocket. Eyeing him more closely I saw his eyes twinkle joyfully while they expressed the contradictory emotion of sorrow. I felt the need to speak to him. I wanted to speak with him, but felt I would be intruding. It was he who spoke first.

"Good afternoon, young man!" He said with a resonant voice that sounded younger than his appearance. "How are you on this fine day?" For once I was at a loss for words. A long minute passed until I realized that I was trying to formulate some response that would not sound foolish.

"Would you like to read part of this newspaper?" he asked indicating the jumbled mass of newsprint in his lap.

"No, thank you. I have read three of them already and have found very little useful information in any of them."

"Yes, that seems to be the way it is. Everything repeats endlessly with slight variations on some ambiguous theme."

"Why do we keep on reading them I wonder?"

"Habit."

"Yes, we anticipate something grand will happen and things will change for the better . . . but they don't." The stranger smiled and nodded. A few minutes later he rose, said 'goodbye' as if we had known each other for years. That feeling had entered my mind and as he walked away I felt that we would meet again. That proved to be true. He appeared almost every day and joined me on the same bench in the park.

Another habit I surmised. But there was something about him that seemed oddly compelling and we met many times thereafter, sitting on the same bench each time. Our conversations expanded into many areas that are seldom trampled over by other people, so it was no surprise that 'our chats' wandered in a discussion of what might be called the inner world. More surprisingly he spoke not only of an inner world, but as if he were speaking from it. He taught me an appreciation of the nebulous existence of this inner world, which I had simply confused with my ego, that self-centered nature of my personality. Fate must have drawn me to him. Or him to me. Perhaps it was something else. Perhaps some unseen powers of the universe were responsible.

At the time of our meetings I was still a relatively young man, but I was not foolish enough to believe anything without evidence of some kind. But some things he alleged irritated me, causing me to grow skeptical. Yet I wanted to hear him out for reasons that I could not fathom. We met regularly as if it was an essential act, somehow necessary for me. And also for him. At times he startled me when he abruptly appeared despite the fact that I was scanning the street looking for him. Sitting with him I became aware of many unrelated thoughts that gnawed away at my self-assurance. I occasionally looked up to see him peering at me with keen intensity. His appearance in my life was somewhat like a premeditated shock.

It was as if he had been sent to stir up my mind, to challenge me somehow. At times he appeared almost bizarre and if I were not rational, I might say that he had suddenly dropped in from some other planet, for there was something about him that seemed timeless yet strangely complete.

It was impossible to determine his age. His appearance   changed from time to time. It was as if he could will those fluctuations like a chameleon. At times he appeared to be 'old.' Then suddenly he was 'younger.' He was polite, seldom displaying anger, or raising his voice even when making observations about people and events that he obviously found distasteful. The anger he occasionally displayed appeared to be an act of some kind, intended strictly for effect.

To describe him accurately is difficult because he seemed different from moment to moment while maintaining an aura of equanimity. His temper and manner were not characteristic of our times. His temper was even, balanced, tranquil. His presence exuded the feeling that he was in absolute control of himself, and his ego, something that we all think is true about ourselves. Although with us, it surely must be illusion. There was a steadiness about him. If the world came apart at any given moment and disintegrated into particles floating off into space he would accept it without qualm.

He was interested and knowledgeable about an endless array of things. His views of life was broad, his thinking capacity was immense. It did not matter if it was a trifling detail or a major event reported in the daily news, his attention and knowledge of it became total. And he possessed an unfailing sincerity. His concentration was remarkable and his level of knowledge was greater than the most astute of my multi-degreed colleagues at the university. He provided information and cogent thought integral to every issue, some that we had previously discussed or of those we were discussing at any given moment.

His memory was superb. The information and ideas that he expressed led our discussions into ever-widening areas of related fields, telescoping views onto the multi-levels of physical and psychological existence, the world around us and the endless universe beyond. Words were like pebbles thrown into a pond creating ripples rolling off in every direction before vanishing into an occasional silence. His thoughts rejoined in the most interesting way, always searching for elusive truths. It was as if the entire universe was available for me to know and understand in my limited way while listening to him. Once I asked him what he was called and as soon as the words left my mouth I realized that they were not appropriate.

"Some call me a charlatan . . . some call me a fool and some question my sanity," he said with a laugh as his eyes twinkled even more. He pronounced his name clearly. It sounded foreign and I told him mine. Thereafter he called me by my surname, Dexter. He seemed to like my name and it rolled off his tongue with a positive élan. He told of his many trips to many countries around the world and said he liked this one very much.

Occasionally we wandered to a nearby café to mix coffee with our conversation. Once I found myself staring at him dumbfounded and bewildered. I had become aware of the feeling that I was with a mystical creature that had chosen to descend to earth. When he predicted the death of a well-known public figure that currently was a picture of robust health, I laughed nervously, expecting him to predict my own death. Suddenly he looked right at me and said, "Do not fear, I am not going to predict your demise!" How did he know that I was thinking that? Yet his prediction about the celebrity proved to be correct for that occurred a few days later.

At my age I rarely through of death, especially my own. Strangely enough, the thought of dying occurred quite often after that, and yet it was never again disconcerting as it had been before. One day after we met, he offered a vivid description of a recent archaeological discovery that had taken place in some remote part of the globe. From that report he segued into several philosophical perspectives, each dealing with some aspect of the possible meanings of life, some as those natives of that remote culture might have interpreted it during that long forgotten age. That led him to reprise our previous discussion during which I displayed my tendency toward nihilism. He carefully and politely destroyed all the salient points with which I had concluded our discussion the day before.

What was truly amazing was that although I had always taken great satisfaction in organizing my arguments, and often took umbrage when someone bested me with words, I found myself readily accepting his comments and rebuttals. It was as though he was doing me a great service. Then I gradually became aware of an almost mysterious sense of tranquility whenever I was in his company; astonished to realize that I had not been aware of such moments to any degree before. I asked him once to write down his thoughts so that others might benefit from his ideas.

"Each being must find its own way . . . each being must find its own truths," he said, "And there are many." He emphasized the word 'being.' "No one can make anyone else truly understand anything, but people can be brainwashed as they say. Most are not aware of their own suggestibility. Most are convinced that they have all the knowledge necessary, all that they will ever need. To really understand life fully and to appreciate the mysteries of life requires more patience than most humans can muster. Illusions and false beliefs are prevalent. They become barriers to understanding . . . truths must be experienced directly and one needs to try to understand all and everything."

Then he made a sweeping gesture that seemed to take in not only our view of the city, but also the universe and the cosmos beyond. "And you must learn to understand with this and this working together," he continued, touching his forehead with one hand and tapping his chest with the other, "You must do that while living as the conscious being that is possible for you, at some level that you are unaware of at this time."

"But what does that mean?" I asked, "And how am I to do that?" He looked at me intently for a moment and smiled, "The problem is not your ignorance. It is your approach, your supposed goals, what you 'think' they might be or what you 'think' they should be. You want a simple answer, some magic formula to that which is complex. Life . . .existence. . .being need to be discovered, appreciated, and known on many levels, but you, Dexter, desire a slogan you can paste in your mind with which you can parade your intelligence around in front of others. The greater part of you wants to stop searching for that which is worthy of the effort required. To be a seeker is difficult. To find, and to know, your real self, and to live from that instead of the nebulous concepts that rule and command you now should be your aim, now and always, everywhere."

Then for a period of time, he failed to appear either at our favorite bench or at our favorite café, and I began to think that he might have been taken ill. After all he was an old man. I remembered that he always appeared quite healthy despite his age, always exuding extraordinary energy. It enveloped him like an aura. Now his absence created an unexplainable void, although oddly enough, I did not feel any dependence upon him. But his words and his presence gave me a different perspective and a subtle transformation took place. Then one day after nonchalantly wandering to our favorite bench expecting him to saunter up momentarily, I quickly disappeared into a maze of thoughts. Gradually they faded away as I grew aware of what could only be described as a true feeling.

I was able to concentrate more deeply than ever and I experienced a dimension of what could only be described as an intense form of attention. It was dynamic, focusing sharply when I relaxed and let it be. Everything became clear. Everything was brighter. Sights, sounds, and each thought that I chose to consider now were observed with greater clarity. I drifted into a quiet place within while I was engulfed in warm sunshine and a soft mellow breeze. I closed my eyes momentarily and when I opened them I saw him shuffling toward me. He appeared like some weather-beaten old man. He sat with a grunt, slouching on the bench next to me. He was silent for a moment before explaining that he had visited a friend who was extremely ill.

I tried to disguise my excitement, and suddenly a torrent of words spewed from my mouth. I found myself babbling a litany of trivialities until I grew aware that my voice and words lacked sincerity, sounding like a hollow reed . . . coarse. . .shrill. I felt foolish and ridiculous. He did not interrupt my posturing, but when I looked into his eyes I felt an incredible sadness. My babbling stopped. I woke up. He said nothing, and yet something in me knew that he was neither upset nor dismayed by my foolishness. It was as if his voice came from within me, "It is all right. I understand that you have been concerned . . . I know and appreciate your feelings."

We sat quietly for several minutes. The words had ceased tumbling from my lips without conscious effort on my part. I felt myself surrender to the experience of his presence. Then his appearance gradually altered. Initially he had sat slouched over but now he was quite erect. He appeared to have regained his normal vitality. His energy grew but now I had an urge to nap, and it occurred to me that he had somehow borrowed energy from me without harming me. Energy had passed between us. I recalled that this feeling happened several times in the past, and perhaps in those prior meetings he may have given me additional energy, an idea that was astonishing and absurd.

I became aware that my body had grown tense, so I relaxed and leaned back sensing myself in a different way. He spoke softly. Perhaps his voice came from within me again. He spoke of an event that occurred to him sometime during the past, but it was as if it were happening at this very moment.

"Several years ago I experienced something unusual, slightly amazing, and slightly bizarre. At first I had difficulty believing that it was happening at all. I had finished my work early one afternoon on a warm spring day, a day much like this one, and I decided to go for a walk . . . to stretch my muscles . . . to empty my mind, and so forth. This took place in a large city of the country in which I was living at the time, before I came to this country. It was relatively quiet, as quiet as a city can be during a busy day of the week. I walked briskly along the street, simply enjoying the warmth of the sun and the fresh smells that followed a sudden shower. It was very pleasant. And as I strolled past the many stores, I watched the reflections appearing in the large glass windows lining the sidewalk. There was the automobile traffic behind me, and a parcel of humanity, people walking along the sidewalk in both directions.

"I saw my own reflection, struck by how clear it and the others were. They appeared to be more real than the actual people and things they reflected. Pleased by my own healthy appearance, and gladdened by the vital figure looking back at me, I smiled back at my reflection, that vibrant man returning my gaze and following me down the boulevard. I mused on the wonder and fullness of life . . . the tranquility of being . . . and I sincerely wished that all people everywhere could experience at some time during their lives the joy which I felt at that moment.

"Near an intersection I paused to look in the window of a haberdashery. There was a suit much like the one I was wearing at the time, neatly arranged on a mannequin whose frozen grin smiled at me through the glass. Then my reflection turned and moved back in the direction from which I had come while I had not moved at all. It no longer seemed to be a reflection at all!

"It was startling to say the least. I slowly turned to see that the figure, bearing every feature that I possessed, was now walking away from me. Yet it was me. This observation did not seem frightening. It seemed real and natural. There I was watching myself walking away while I stood still watching its movement. It crossed the street. So I did something that was appropriate and necessary, I crossed the street and followed the image walking along. I fully expected to encounter it sooner or later and I began to rehearse in my mind what I would say to it when I at last would confront it."

He paused for a few minutes, scrutinizing my face for signs of the doubt he expected to see there. But I found myself absorbed in the story even as my mind was humming arguments against accepting it as being true. Those thoughts were crowded out by a strange sensation in the pit of my stomach not caused by physical hunger. It must have been a different kind of hunger. We sat without talking for several minutes while I desperately wanted to ask him what had happened next.

What would he say to the apparition? But my tongue refused to move as questions circled in my head like vultures reveling at a feast. The idea came to me that I might be imagining everything that he had just said. Perhaps everything that he said before, all our previous conversations were also merely my imagination. Surely that was possible. These ideas joined other negative thoughts racing through my mind, but all of them eventually disappeared only after a difficult struggle. Other things then appeared. There were instructions, and a gentle tug on my sleeve. A voice told me to sit quietly and to wait. Was it the wind, or did he touch me? I do not know. It was a gentle force. So I obeyed.

Finally he rose, bid me good day, as he had done many times before, and sauntered off in the direction from which he came, now moving with an elegant stride. I sat there after returning his farewell. Then a peaceful feeling which cannot be described again came over me. My thoughts were focused, centering on perceptions of myself in the context of the world around me. I sat there for a long time pondering his story.

It was hard for me to believe, but I wanted to believe it. But there is more. There is always more. An idea took shape in my mind. I decided to test the story somehow. But the immediate problem of how to test the truth of anything that seemed so preposterous loomed before me. It was only a few days later that I was able to return to our bench with an idea in mind.

I sat quietly. A slight breeze arose. It seemed as if there was a tug on my sleeve again, but there was no one there. After several minutes some unknown force compelled me to rise, and to walk across the street and stroll along the several shops. I felt slightly foolish as I grew aware of the many reflections from store windows as I wandered along. The reflections were of the people walking by, the automobiles moving past, and the dazzling greenness of the trees in the park across the way from which I had come contrasting with the bright blueness above. There were large puffy clouds reflected, high above in a sky, bright and pleasant as the sun beamed down between them.

I walked on for several minutes, expecting, and even daring my reflection to separate from me and walk in the opposite direction. Something in me expected that to happen. But it did not. It was disappointing. I tried to conjure up an image of myself beckoning to me from across the street. The more I tried the more frustrating and useless it became. When nothing happened I decided to give up on what surely was an insane quest.

I retraced my steps, crossed the boulevard heading back to the park and our favorite bench, wanting a quiet place to sit. As I approached the curbing I stumbled and fell, laying there for several moments unable to move. A few good Samaritans offered assistance. Others seeing how young I was may have thought that I was inebriated and moved away. A kind policeman helped me to my feet. I now felt even more foolish and angered by my own inattention. I wanted to laugh aloud as I remembered that I was in the act of looking for myself instead of watching where I was stepping. What would these people think if they knew what exactly I had been trying to accomplish?

The dull pain in my right leg accompanied me as I limped to the empty bench, slumping onto it breathlessly, where I sat stiffly with my eyes closed. After a few minutes a very pleasant serenity came over me, a wonderful sense of being. That replaced my self-centered desire to prove myself right. For a moment I thought this sensation must be what dying is like. I was free. But it also was perplexing. I didn't wish to experience thoughts of death. Instead I began to ponder again my enigmatic friend's story. When I opened my eyes I glanced across the street.

And so it happened. I saw it. There was the figure of a man limping along, now moving just past the greengrocer. My vision seemed to blur. Tears welled up my eyes but I stubbornly held them back. Why should I cry? What was the reason for that? I did not understand. I wiped my eyes in wonderment, and sat upright squinting, trying to see more clearly. What? There were no doubts in my mind now, or my heart, which was beating inside my chest, throbbing in unison with the dull pain in my leg. It was true. I was looking at myself over there across the street, limping along, pausing occasionally to look into shop windows before moving on. Yet here I was sitting on a park bench across the street, a good distance away. Then after the figure moved out of sight I began seeing images of myself during various times of my life.

They flashed by in frightening scenes like those one would see in a horror movie. Some of the scenes were unflattering, some so disgusting and disturbing that I wanted to turn away. Yet I was compelled to watch. A strong taste of vomit appeared deep in my throat. Fortunately other scenes appeared that were joyful and pleasant.

All the while my gaze remained transfixed. I had stared with disbelief and often with horror at the unpleasant scenes. It was like viewing my own soul, and the insanity of many of my actions and attitudes. All of this occurred with a resounding force such as I had never before experienced. The sight of each transgression and stupidity committed during my life was appalling. I experienced shame and sorrow. More disturbing was that a part of me thought all of this was appropriate and even necessary.

I now understood that all those thoughts and actions had been necessary and essential to my existence. That was what I had been. The question remained as to what I was now, what I might become. While part of me wished to turn away again and again, another part cherished each image. Time stopped. The great horror of the past froze in my mind, and seared my soul. Then something else strange occurred.

"Who are you?" said a strange voice that seemed to emanate somewhere around me.

"Why, I am . . . you!" said another voice that sounded far away yet seemingly hovered nearby.

"What do you want? . . . why are you here? . . .why did you come?" I managed in a hoarse whisper.

"You have been looking for me for a long time."

"I cannot believe this! . . . this cannot be happening!"

"You need not believe anything . . . you need not do anything, and what is more, you really cannot do anything."

"You are not at all like what I had imagined you to be!" I stammered, as I looked around frantically for the source of the voices. But, alas, I was alone there on the bench.

"Would you prefer that I exist like one of the many illusions that have gripped you from time to time . . . those vapid pretensions that you so ably concocted and you so carefully executed over and over again?"

"Yes! . . . no!. . . oh my God! . . . I don't know!" Street sounds were muted, far away now in some other world beyond me. Tensions in my body gradually dissipated as I sensed the air moving in and out of my lungs. I repeated one of my questions.

"What do you want?" I pleaded. My mind wandered into strange thoughts. Was all of this a strange epiphany or an even more unimaginable apotheosis? I did not know. The voice had only a few more words for me which it spoke softly.

"Just . . . *be!*"

Buenos Notches

Lost and confused, Bailey hurried along over what appeared to be a large campus He realized that at this moment he was supposed to be in a class somewhere. But where were his books? Like a dumb-bell, he had forgotten them, and his rooming house was several blocks away so there wasn't enough time to go back for them. So he began to jog along not sure of where he was going while others walking along seemed confident of their destination, and yet Bailey was afraid to ask them for directions. It was unsettling looking around at everything that seemed vaguely familiar yet oddly different.

He stopped. It dawned on him that he did not remember which class he was supposed to be attending. And he didn't know which room in what building that unknown class was taking place. He was sure of one thing though; he hadn't read any of the assigned materials, whatever they were. His mind searched unsuccessfully for answers to these questions as he approached a large parking lot.

His attention shifted. He began looking for his car although he didn't know why. He was certain that he did not own an automobile, at least not yet. Still he searched for it. Where was it? Why couldn't he find it? He wandered through several rows of parked vehicles, and his car wasn't anywhere among them. But then he wasn't sure what kind of car it was that he was looking for. It must be stolen he reasoned, and should be reported to the police. In the distance bells in a tower tolled the hour. He looked at the watch on his wrist, but it had no hands on its face. Then something unbelievable occurred. Bailey found himself soaring high above looking down and marveling at the tops of the trees below him.

Somehow he was able to avoid the power lines that often loomed up just ahead. He smiled to himself as his body floated effortlessly, rising and descending at will. It all seemed quite natural. None of this bothered him in the least. He forgot the stolen car. He forgot the missing textbooks. He forgot about missing his class. Yet in a corner of his mind he became aware he was dreaming. He must be. Gradually the sense of gliding through the air and the panoramic view faded, disappearing into a quiet darkness where only a chirping sound could be heard.

Bailey opened his eyes as rays of the morning sun came through an open window near his bed. The light splayed over the Spartan furnishings of the room. Beyond the open window birds were singing a cheery welcome to another day. He lay quietly in bed, having forgotten the dreams that had absorbed him moments ago. He closed his eyes for several minutes and lay there listening. Off in the distance mourning doves cooed softly, seeking their mates. He propped himself up on one elbow, and squinted toward an aide who had poked her head through the doorway asking him if he needed assistance in dressing. He waved her off with a grunt, rose from the bed, put on a bathrobe, and shuffled mechanically to the bathroom, conscious again of the strange feeling of dread that appeared in him frequently. Much too frequently he thought. It hung in the air around him for several days like a sickening vapor. Or was it weeks? It was a feeling that something was drastically wrong, but he had no idea of what that could be. Perhaps it was his illness, or the many pills he swallowed each day. His doctors said he was in remission, and that there was nothing to worry about.

Still a faint lingering guilt haunted him, which he tried to understand, and if not, he wanted it to simply disappear. At times nothing seemed to make sense anyway. He was resigned to his predicament. Life never made much sense to him, especially now. Yet several thoughts passed through his mind during breakfast, which he ate in a half-empty dining room. Many of the patients were immobile, and meals were taken to their rooms.

As he mulled through those endless thoughts, he began to realize that he had been unprepared for most of the things that happened during his life. Despite his age he was unprepared for his retirement as well as the death of his wife, and his grown children moving away, scattered in various parts of the country. One of them killed in Korea. He was definitely unprepared for the cancer that brought him here for 'rehabilitation.'

After breakfast he went outside to sit on the patio near his room. There was a pleasant view. The well-kept ground resembled a college campus. It gave the place its name – Shady Green Acres. Leaning back he wondered if he was ready for what lay ahead. After all he was approaching eighty. Fewer days were ahead of him than had already slipped away behind him into those shadows of the past. Then nostalgic thoughts of his childhood returned. Not all memories were pleasant however.

He was seven when a neighborhood boy was accidentally killed while hunting. The boy leaned his shotgun against a fence while climbing over it. The shotgun discharged into his groin killing him instantly. Custom at that time was to display the body for viewing in the parlor at home. Bailey was taken to view the body. It lay in a coffin surrounded by the pungent odor of the many floral arrangements that filled the room. The smell sickened him, and he grew to dislike the smell of flowers, even the noxious earthy odor wafting from the open door of a greenhouse he passed on his way to school.

A few years later another a younger boy from his neighborhood was struck and killed by an automobile while running into its path. Bailey was assigned to be one of pallbearers much against his will. For him it had been a traumatic experience to say the least. Each pallbearer wore white gloves as if death were contagious. These experiences magnified his fears. While walking home from school he occasionally passed a funeral home and always avoided walking close to the open door of the ominous looking hearse parked at the curb. Surely death would reach out and pull him kicking and screaming into its purple velvet interior and carry him off to hell.

Bailey had spent most of his life as an accountant for a large corporation. Against his better judgment he had been party to 'cooking the books' a few times. He regretted doing that, but it was either that or losing his job. He had other regrets as well. He had a few affairs knowledge of which he was able to keep from his wife. But then she was a product of Victorian thinking with regard to sexual intimacy, concentrating upon being a housewife and mother. Conjugal activity was a duty, and consequently she performed it in a stilted manner, unable to engage in it for sheer pleasure. Then there were the children, who despite his counsel grew up to be money chasers. For them money was everything. Little else mattered to them.

His reverie ended, he went inside into the near empty lounge where he pulled out the checkerboard hoping an opponent would materialize. The last two disappeared for good as did others at the home. Their bodies were spirited away before breakfast in an unmarked van, perhaps to avoid upsetting the rest of the 'inmates,' as he thought of them and himself. It was as if those who departed had never existed, and there was little mention of them afterward. As he placed the checkers, he tried to remember their names but couldn't. Looking out a window, lost in thought, he was unaware of a newcomer who had entered and was sitting nearby. Finally the stranger put down the newspaper he had been reading and turned to him.

"Checkers?"

"Sure, why not, it'll help pass the time." The man moved to the table and sat opposite Bailey.

"Which color do you want?"

"It doesn't matter. Fate always takes its course."

"You sound philosophical."

"Call me Aaron, my name is Aaron Dexter; I just got here last night, so I need to adjust to the surroundings."

"Bailey. . .Bailey Callahan. Don't call me Bail, or 'Old Bailey!' Been here five weeks. You can move first if you like."

The game commenced. An occasional grunt or sigh took the place of words, and they soon became absorbed in the game. The sound of the checkers hitting the surface of the board punctuated their sporadic conversation.

"What's this place like?" asked Aaron.

"It's okay I guess, but they ought to call it assisted dying instead of assisted living." Then after a short pause, "We're lucky to be walking though, I guess, but if we were in wheelchairs like most of the others around here, we could always drag-race down the hallways until they made us stop!"

"Most of them seem to be drugged."

"Yeah, they're out of it, luckily for them, huh?"

"What are you in for?" asked Aaron.

"Cancer."

"Oh, damn! What kind?"

"Colon. They tell me I'm in remission."

"My wife had pancreatic. . .six months."

"Mine had that. Lasted about the same. What brought you here besides qualifying for the golden age crowd?"

"Heart. My daughter lives in New York, and I am alone since my wife died. The doctor said I needed someone to make sure I take my pills on schedule."

Bailey nodded. He and Aaron played almost every day for several weeks. Their conversation gradually grew as time went on. At first Bailey disliked his new partner who had a preference for chess, a highbrow game if ever there was one. Aaron also seemed kind of stuffy. He was too intelligent; too smart for his own good, using big words that Bailey interpreted as some high-brow affectation. Yet, there was something about Aaron that was appealing. He was sincere. Not many like that in the business world, thought Bailey. Over time, they developed a rapport and Bailey grew to like his new checkers partner.

Out of the blue one day, Bailey saw that he had developed an unusual trust in Aaron. He couldn't explain why or how that happened. But he realized that Aaron knew a good deal about everything, and he talked intelligently about everything. Bailey saw that Aaron, despite his great knowledge, talked with him, not down at him. That drew Bailey out his self-centeredness and he soon surprised himself by discovering that he could respond to Aaron's thoughts and ideas intelligently. So their friendship grew, something that surprised them both, because they held differing opinions about almost everything involving politics, religion, and economics. Bailey aggressively supported the idea of warfare. Something Aaron described as futile and a blot on mankind's history.

Bailey had not served in the military due to a punctured ear drum, but Aaron had been an intelligence officer with the Third Army in Europe during the Second World War and had been privy to a great deal of classified information. He had knowledge of many tactical and strategic errors committed by field officers, some of which resulted in the ever-growing number of casualties, the necessary cost of war due to the chaos of battle and the pride of warriors.

"Do you realize that the costs of all the wars during only the last century could have practically rid the entire world of poverty and disease? Poverty and its consequential ignorance are two of humanity's greatest curses, matched only by a colossal stupidity shared by many people with their political leaders. And the offspring of poverty and ignorance is injustice," said Aaron who had taught history and philosophy before retiring to Shady Green Acres. After a pause, he continued.

"But worse still is that many people suffer from a poverty of spirit. And what is absolutely disillusioning is the flagrant ignorance among the educated people of the world."

A sharp pain erupted in Bailey's side. He grimaced but said nothing.

"You okay?" Aaron inquired.

"Yeah." He changed the subject, "So your ticker is bad, huh?"

"They say I could go anytime now."

"You don't sound like you're afraid."

"Someone once wrote that the fear of death is greater than death itself. Perhaps it is poetic justice that many of the most rabid believers in heaven are often the most fearful of dying."

"Don't tell me that you don't believe in the hereafter?"

"No."

"No?" Bailey leaned forward to study the face of his friend, Aaron. He didn't look like an atheist. Then after a moment he wondered what an atheist was like. He had to ask.

"What's it like to be an atheist?"

"I didn't say I didn't believe in anything."

"Well, what do you think about the hereafter?"

"Oh, there will be a hereafter but I won't be here."

"Where then?"

"I haven't the foggiest. Perhaps you can consider me to be agnostic. But it isn't likely that I will be singing somewhere on a cloud up there playing a harp or anything like that. Perhaps what's left of my consciousness, if any of it survives, will unite with a greater consciousness in space somewhere out there in the universe."

"Isn't that a kind of heaven?"

"Not like the advertised kind," Aaron looked pensive for a moment, "It's fairly certain that there are various forces continually operating and maintaining the universe, and although I consider myself an intelligent being, I admit to not understanding the mystery of the origins of life."

"Why do you see yourself in the universe?"

"Well, it obviously exists. And we must be in it. I must be of it, and meanwhile science is forever working to learn more about it. But a corpse oxidizes over time, you know, ashes to ashes."

"Maybe science and religion can reconcile their diametrically opposed positions."

"I doubt it," than after a pause, "For an accountant you sure come up with some interesting observations."

"Well, I've read more than balance sheets and profit and loss statements. I've always been fascinated by things that don't add up, especially what happens to us after we die."

"You could be the character out of James Joyce who spoke of metempsychosis."

"Metam . . .what? What the hell is that?"

"Transmigration of the soul. But that raises the question of what the soul might be composed of, what it truly might be, and what it's like. Maybe we simply aren't given one as has been thought. Maybe we each have to grow one, if that is possible. Maybe that is our purpose in life, and yet it appears that many, if not all, people don't think of that, and if they do, they don't know how to go about it."

"Oh, that's a far out idea . . . crown my king over there."

"Not really. It's been around for centuries . . .the transmigration part. Lot's of disagreement about when and how a soul is formed. In another vein, you could say that man is simply not complete. He needs to evolve psychologically."

"You don't pray? Go to church?"

"Used to. Hardly ever now. But it's likely that everyone prays either consciously or subconsciously, especially when serious illness or trouble appears. Many probably pray only when they want something. But I'm not sure a heaven or hell exists elsewhere. I lean toward the poet Blake's idea who said both heaven and hell are right here on earth."

"That makes sense. But you don't buy a life hereafter?"

"I simply don't know. Suppose there is no god. Suppose the one we were told of was developed by the imagination of frightened men, our earliest ancestors. That may be the kind religion speaks of . . . its apotheosis . . .man humanized god and his devil making them persons so they could be understood. But faith and reason don't blend well. Faith is not the same as religion. Faith is the belief in something greater than oneself, some higher powers, and knowing that the universe was not created for one individual, or for one world for that matter. Religion for the most part consists of dogmatic assertions that are accepted by the pious and those pretending to be pious. Many of them are conditioned to fear death, and that may include the bulk of the population. However, religion serves a social purpose and helps to keep people in line, sort of a brake on their habits and unruly inclinations. But I believe that all we may be able to do is accept our lot, love life, all life, everywhere, and when the time comes, simply say goodbye."

"Do all of your ideas come out of your experience with teaching history and philosophy?"

"Not really, but years ago when I was younger I met a man who gave me a kind of park bench education."

"How so?"

"He said that it wasn't how you think, or what you think, but rather what you think with, what he called the complete self. One needs to work toward perfection of being despite the fact that it may be unattainable. Then I've grown to accept the many forces that govern the universe, and thus our planet and all the people and things on it. Two major forces are constructive and destructive. It may be that the friction and the tension between them cause life forms to appear. Perhaps the good and evil are simply these forces acting ad infinitum, ad nauseam."

Aaron went on to describe the need for some reconciling force in order that harmony and equilibrium may materialize. All three, he said seem to be essential and responsible for the existence of the universe, and all the life in it. He was quite willing to accept the idea that those forces were 'God' in some way, but certainly not the God that man had invented.

"Mankind muddles its way through life, and life muddles its way around and through mankind. To revere and honor life may be the highest purpose for mankind, especially those who have developed what could be called true individuality. Maybe the purpose of life is simply to seek a purpose of some kind. Maybe more than one even. Who can say which is truly right or wrong?

"But imagine a world without religion. Somebody would have to invent one quickly because people need to believe in something. That is an extremely strong instinct, perhaps connected to the survival instinct. Imagine what the first humans needed to endure, the many great unknowns, all those forces in the universe playing out around them. They faced and feared extinction. They sought answers. They looked around at each other, then finally up at the sun, the moon, and the stars. That's were those forces seemed to be coming from."

All of this fascinated Bailey who had clung to religion most of his life, but gradually slipped away from its power. He no longer feared or needed it. He was upset when ministers at funerals intoned, "He's in a better place now." How in hell did they know? Bailey never thought being dead was such a good idea, except to end a painful struggle with a terminal disease. But now he noticed something different since Aaron and he played checkers. That feeling of dread which followed him for weeks like a plague was absent whenever he was with Aaron who once said that we live only as long as we have some purpose.

"Life ends when there is no longer any need for us," and he predicted that in the future, perhaps the distant future, man would no longer need dogmatic religions after he had learned to accept his mortality. But ignorance and superstition had a powerful grip on the human psyche. "There is some kind of a transcendental spirituality permeating throughout the universe, and maybe man will discover some of that long after you and I are gone."

Their checkers games and their many conversations affected Bailey deeply. He began sleeping each night now without those annoying dreams. One afternoon they were playing when Bailey thought of a question that he wanted to ask, but he was reluctant to ask. But finally he blurted it out at their next meeting.

"Are you afraid of dying, Aaron?"

"No, are you Bailey?"

"I think so . . . yes. . . shit yes . . . maybe I am."

"There were cultures where the fear of death failed to make inroads and grow because of a different kind of thinking. It was believed by certain American Indian tribes that an old brave could actually choose the day he would die."

"Why would they do that? Were they real old. . . or just plain didn't give a damn?"

"Age was part of the equation. They felt that it was time to die when they understood that their purpose in life had been completed, and that there was nothing more for them to do. Their presence was no longer needed. When they experienced this sense of completion, they simply ate a nice supper, went outdoors, sat down and leaned against a tree and watched the sun go down at the end of the day. When it disappeared from view beyond the horizon, they closed their eyes and accepted death."

"How do we know that our purpose is complete? Hell, I'm of no use to anybody anymore! What am I hanging around for? Is it just because of my fear?"

"Perhaps, or maybe you have something yet to contribute."

"What could I contribute? To who? You're the only one I really know around here and you sure don't need my help! What can I give you besides crowning one of your checkers when it gets over to my side," said Bailey with a laugh.

"Opportunities often come unexpectedly."

They played several more times until one day when Aaron failed to appear in the dinning room for breakfast. Bailey was concerned, but not upset when he learned of his friend's fate. He made inquiry, and a short time later an aide came to tell him that Aaron had passed away that morning before breakfast.

"What happened? What did he say?" asked Bailey.

"At dawn he looked up at me, smiled, and then he said 'Goodbye' and closed his eyes. That was it." She said.

Bailey sat quietly for a long time thinking about Aaron and their unusual rapport. He remembered his friend clearly, and was neither surprised nor shocked, and oddly enough he didn't feel the need to grieve. He somehow felt Aaron's presence all through the following days as he recalled their many checker games. Bailey religiously set up the checkerboard each day as if he expected Aaron or another one like him to walk in at any moment. But an opponent didn't appear for some time.

A few weeks had passed when another type of man sauntered into the lounge one afternoon. Bailey introduced himself, and invited the man to play checkers.

"Gordon Chapman is my name! Everybody calls me Jake 'cause I sure in hell wouldn't stand anybody callin' me 'Gordy,' or 'Chappy,' or some half-assed name like that! Shit, if somebody did, I'd punch out their lights!" Chapman looked and spoke like a cowboy, something he had been for a short time earlier in his life. That role appealed to him, and he relished playing it even now. Chapman had recently retired after driving a city bus for twenty-five years. He spoke with the rasping voice, and often coughed deeply, relics of his smoking habit.

"What you in fur?"

Bailey told him about his own battle with cancer only to learn that Jake too was fighting cancer, lung cancer. And Jake's prognosis was not too good. Checkers now became a part of his life, taking him away from thoughts of his illness that plagued him in the same manner as that peculiar dread had plagued Bailey. Jake also liked to boast, and poke fun at others. He had a streak of meanness that surfaced from time to time.

Bailey sat quietly and overlooked Jake's tendency to cheat while Jake provided a lurid account of his life, dwelling primarily on the many women he had seduced with the help of liquor and lies. To Jake they were like prizes. He remembered each raucous conquest, vividly describing several of his fornication scenes in great detail. This amused Bailey and he saw the enormous contrast between Gordon Chapman and Aaron Dexter.

What a horse's ass, thought Bailey. But he was not surprised several days later during one afternoon when the boisterous loud talking cowboy disappeared to be replaced by a worried-looking and very frightened Jake Chapman. He had been extremely quiet during the two games that they had already played. Something was bothering him a great deal. That was apparent to Bailey who wondered what it could be. Jake's cancer was growing worse. That was it, Bailey thought. Finally Jake mustered up the courage to ask about something that had been on his mind for days.

"You 'fraid a dyin', Bailey?"

The question caught Bailey off-guard, and he had to think for a few moments before responding. Silence was a friend. There was something in the corner of his brain that was pushing, trying to come forth. So he sat thinking for a few minutes trying to remember something that seemed to be at the tip of his tongue but refused to take form. Then he remembered what Aaron said about death. He looked pensively at Jake now as he spoke.

"Yeah," he said, "We all are, aren't we? But you believe in God and heaven, don't you?

"Sure, I do," Jake responded, almost in a whisper as tears began to fill his eyes. "But I've been such a bad-ass most my life that I kin expect the worst now, cain't I? Been such a hell raiser and now I'm heading straight for hell ain't I? Ain't I?"

He was breathing hard and almost broke down except that a portion of his cowboy nature clung to him and would not allow him to show more emotion than he had already exhibited. He had suffered through the night before a doctor came to administer a sedative. Truth was that cancer had reappeared in Jake's lungs as Bailey suspected. Bailey sat quietly for a few moments gathering his thoughts as he studied Jake's eyes, which displayed the look of terror.

"Listen," Bailey spoke calmly, "God will forgive you all of that. All you got to do is be sorry for having raised so much hell and you'll be forgiven. And when you go, why, you'll go straight up to heaven like all the other folks!" The room was silent, but Jake's appearance slowly changed.

Jake was smiling now, "You really think so?" I mean, that makes me feel so much better 'n maybe I kin sleep good tonight! Been havin' trouble getting' shut-eye since I got here. Lots of bad dreams! In some of them the devil asking for me!"

"Take it easy . . . king my guy over there!"

Jake was relieved, and began to smile even more as he placed a checker on the one Bailey had moved to the last row.

"Thanks a heap, old man . . . you done me a big favor!"

The color returned to Jake's cheeks. He relaxed, and his worrisome nature slowly vanished. His cowboy act returned with gusto as they played. Several weeks passed. Then Jake passed away quietly one night. Autumn approached with gusting winds that made fallen leaves dance wildly across the spacious lawns. The landscape changed; trees were transferring their glory from one season to another.

A few days later Bailey enjoyed supper. Afterward he pulled on a windbreaker and sat in a chair on the patio. There was no one to play checkers with. Perhaps that was the sign. He felt serene viewing the rolling land. Off in the west a majestic sun of brilliant reds and oranges slid beyond the horizon. Bailey leaned back thinking of nothing in particular. Everything was okay. He was at ease with himself. He closed his eyes and slipped effortlessly into the darkness.

Concatenation

THE PARTY WAS GOING full blast by the time he arrived. When he entered the smoke-filled room he was greeted by sounds of clinking glasses. Revelers milled about here, and in several other rooms, each with drink in hand. Some toasted each other, while others mockingly toasted anything and everything. Some munched on cheese and crackers. All of them seemed to be talking at the same time. No one seemed to be listening. No matter. Not much could be heard over the din formed by the constant buzz of excited voices of people intent on enjoying themselves. Those who were not enjoying themselves felt obligated to pretend that they were. Raucous laughter punctuated the cacophony of voices, erupting from one group or another when the punch line of a joke managed to reach someone's ears. Occasionally revelers were drawn to the growing circle around the jokester generating the most laughter.

People milled about pursuing the happiness that for some of them came from the spirits they had liberated from one of the dark bottles lined up on the home-made bar in one corner of the room. The air filled with vapid conversation loaded with the kind of banality common to cocktail parties. Each room in the house echoed with mindless chatter, and those not under the spell of alcohol worked diligently in order to appear blissful and happy. But he stood alone, almost apart from the celebration going on around him and watched it without expression. Convinced that much of the mirth around him was affectation, he observed it with a slight amazement and quiet detachment. Yet it was not for him to change the attitudes of the party-goers. What little of the conversation that could be heard was platitudes and clichés, the kind expected from those whose inhibitions were washed away by excitement and liquor. There was something patently false about cocktail parties he thought, and to him many of the revelers appeared to be trying too hard to be happy, hiding true feelings if they even possessed any. After all, this was a party. One must be happy. What else was one supposed to do?

Now and then mention was made of the reason for the party, the closing night of a stage play of which only a fraction of the revelers had taken part. A handful of actors and backstage workers mingled with hangers-on who desired to brush up against celebrity, even if those celebrities were amateurs. Most of the members of the theater group that produced the play managed to show up for every cast party. Attendance at them had grown to be a ritual with those people regardless of whether or not they attended the performances. And those members usually found ways to absent themselves on workdays when the scenery was being constructed and painted, when their help was needed.

Some avoided volunteering and doing any of the jobs that would get their hands dirty, jobs that lacked the glamour of acting onstage. Applause massaged the ego of performers, but if it was not available to some members of the group, neither were they. Ironically some of them had to be cajoled into taking even plum roles. They found it necessary to posture and boast regardless of their stage abilities and they adroitly faked humility in accepting accolades thrown their way, deserved or not.

The late arrival stood quietly in one corner, feeling that he did not belong here, but he managed to smile and respond to remarks directed at him. Acting was part of his job of directing anyway. Why not here? Although he resented the sham, for some reason he wanted to be part of the celebration. Still he felt a bit sad and lonely despite the throng surrounding him. When those nearby became aware of him they showered him with the usual compliments. His work received a grudging respect from most of the group although there were those who thought that he was overbearing and much too serious about everything.

"Is it true that you want to do some of those crazy kinds of plays from what is called 'Theater of the Absurd?' Those kind of plays you want to do won't sell many tickets around here, you know. Our motto is let the audience go away happy!"

"Sam Beckett's play, Waiting for Godot, is a provocative piece and would be a worthy challenge for any group . . . it speaks to man about what it is to know . . to be . . ."

"Yeah, maybe, but you are too gung-ho for those damned message plays and that stuff gets awfully heavy, not to mention awfully boring. Why put on those kinds of plays, anyway?"

"Yeah, we should do musicals . . . they'll make us more money . . . they're more fun than your Arthur Miller and his 'Death of a Salesman.' That kind of play is too damned morbid for people around here." Such comments spewed from members of the group who had not witnessed the play they were here to celebrate and unable to appreciate its impact on the audience.

Amidst the chattering voices bits of sentimental music filtered through to occupy any space not filled with laughter or loud talk. Noise could mask emptiness. There were moments when he wished he could disappear, but he felt obligated to acknowledge the cast and crew and they would be disappointed if he had not joined them. He merely smiled at those critical of his ideas and his preference for serious drama. His work pleased him, and he was aware of the contributions of each cast member and stage crew. He wanted to remain connected with them somehow.

He had become a student of theater in the broadest sense and had learned how to give meaningful instructions to his actors while growing steadily impatient with the organization.

He studied theater on his own, learning from books and observing both amateur and professional performances. He wanted to know everything all at once, and now regretted not having studied theater at college. Fortunately his faculty adviser, Aaron Dexter introduced him to drama and philosophy and encouraged him to read "Psychology of Being" by Abraham Maslow.

He realized that the occasional heightened feelings he had observed in himself were like those peak experiences Maslow had described. By directing plays he discovered a way to share his feelings and express himself through the words of great playwrights. He became a different person when working with a cast, even able to be patient with actors when needed.

The characters of the play they had just performed were complex and offered a wide range of emotional attitudes for his actors to work and convey to the audience. The many rehearsals resulted in the solid performance which pleased the small, appreciative audience earlier that evening. The conflicts within each of the characters were displayed and resolved. The lyric quality of the script carried the audience through emotions filled with sadness and pathos, but the ending was far from 'happy.' There were few dry eyes in the audience when the final curtain came down.

Such plays were not normal fare for Community Theater. Other directors preferred not to dwell on inner feelings of characters to any degree and grew proficient in staging bedroom farces and wispy comedies relying on sight gags and innuendo. But somehow this drama was chosen, and the empathy conjured on stage was absent in the revelers who preferred drink and idle palaver. Yet his actors needed relief from the powerful emotions generated and experienced by them during the performances.

He felt it was his duty to create a safe environment in the rehearsal hall, allowing the actors to incorporate their own emotions and thoughts with those of their characters while pulling the audience into the play and along the path indicated by the playwright. He outlined this aim at their first meeting, explaining to them that the author had crafted a meaningful story that they would to bring to life. "The author gave us the play," he told them at their first rehearsal, "And I will give it to you during the next few weeks. Then you will then give it to the audience." He promised them that something would happen to each of them that would be satisfying, and of more significance than they might expect.

He looked more like an athlete than a play director, and his natural shyness disappeared during rehearsals where a confidence exuded from him even as he masked his own ambivalent feelings. He understood the contribution of teamwork and spirit generated by a cast and hoped to motivate the actors into reaching beyond themselves to a level of ensemble work. A few actors in each cast usually resisted, preferring to ignore directions they did not like, often sure they needed little direction and relying instead on tricks they had learned in some previous play. Generally those in key roles listened to him. They responded. Others reluctantly, and often unconsciously, followed the example before them, resulting in elevating the level of the entire cast for performances.

Now he grew melancholy watching the revelers as the noise around him increased. Some voices grew loud and shrill. The music blared into a subdued roar somewhere in the background. He felt an emptiness growing inside and loosened his necktie. It was almost like being imprisoned in a world of nonsense. He knew he should stay. At the same time he wanted to get away, if only for a short time. He made his way to the door and slipped quietly out into the night. No one missed his departure.

After quietly closing the door behind him, he stood in the driveway. The din of the party faded, replaced by the silence of a cool evening disturbed only by the barking of a dog a few houses down the street. Occasionally the barking accompanied the sound of an automobile driving past. The quiet night air was refreshing. At least it was devoid of the canopy of blue smoke hanging over every room in the house. He looked up at a bright panorama of stars sprinkling bits of light throughout space. They were far away yet close.

He thought of the interdependence of life, life in its many forms. There were endless connections in body, mind and emotions. Words from a scene in the play came back to him as he watched the stars in the sky. Those words were like dawn's light breaking through the morning fog. Absorbed in this serenity, he did not hear the door open and close until someone emerged from the shadows and stood nearby.

"Got a cigarette?" said a pleasant voice standing close to him. He recognized the voice. It belonged to one of the actors who had a major role in the play. She was an attractive woman who possessed sensitivity and intelligence, characteristics he admired. He liked her immediately when she read at the auditions. She took direction extremely well and occasionally offered useful suggestions from the perspective of her character. That made his work easier. Most amateur actors did neither with regularity, certainly not as frequently. Aware of this bit of affectation, he smiled to himself as he lighted two cigarettes at once as he had seen a character in a movie doing a long time ago.

"You're awfully quiet," she paused to exhale before continuing, "Is there something the matter?"

"No," he said. She joined him looking up at the sky and a few moments passed in silence.

"A penny for your thoughts?" she asked.

"I feel a bit sad because it's over, the play I mean."

"There will be others."

"Maybe...maybe not." He paused for a moment, "I am thinking of quitting this whole thing."

"Oh, don't say that! Without you this group would. . . I mean there's no director around that can do what you do."

"This group will fold up anyway sooner or later."

"Why do you say that?"

"Look at the support, or rather the lack of support that this cast received, and this was one of the better pays. Most of those inside didn't even come to the show tonight. Most of them did not raise a finger to help."

"But the play went well, didn't it?

"Yes."

"Then stop all this talk of quitting!"

"You need to know how difficult it is to get things done . . . to get things necessary for the play to go well. . .and well, I'm getting tired, and I can't do this forever."

"Have you spoken to the board?"

"Yes, we are on different pages when it comes to what our group should, what theater should be. For them it is just another hobby, something to do to kill time much like what most of the folks inside there think sopping up liquor." He took the last drag of his cigarette, snuffed it out under his shoe, and felt her shivering next to him. She was wearing a sleeveless dress, so he removed his jacket and draped it over her shoulders. She stood quietly watching him in the dim light. Then she turned and embraced him. He held her close so the jacket wouldn't slide off her shoulders, relishing the solace of her presence.

It was a tender embrace, more than what siblings would do, but less than what lovers would exchange. Somehow the tension in his body evaporated along with some of his melancholy. He enjoyed the sweetness of her being near. She leaned her head against his shoulder, her hair touching his cheek. Neither spoke for several moments as they stood looking up at the small lights blinking in the sky far away.

She smiled up at him. Then he closed his eyes to savor the moment, and was surprised to feel her lips on his. The moment was very pleasant. He was not demonstrative when it came to his feelings, and it was not his habit to kiss women who acted in his plays. Yet she was special. Thoughts of tomorrow vanished. He enjoyed this moment for it made everything seem worth while.

"You are a very good director. . ."

"Thanks."

". . .you offer insights for each of us while other directors just sit there smoking cigarettes, or reading a magazine. It's almost as if you had written the play . . . you understand the motivations of the characters and it's uncanny how you seem to feel everything they are feeling. Your direction allowed us to bring the play to life for them and for us just as you promised that it would."

Her compliments were welcome, much more so than the contrived accolades others threw his way. Wary of praise, he avoided it while directing, doling out little to his actors, feeling that undue praise blinded and hindered them, preventing them from continuing the search for the depth of character.

"Anyone can direct plays if they pay attention to the words provided ... to the actors ... the details sprinkled throughout the script defining motivations ..."

"Yes, but you bring more than that. You have a great deal of affection for each play, and for each of us. We all feel it."

"My main job is riding herd on a bunch of egos ... including my own," he replied sardonically. Although conscious of his personal feelings during rehearsals, he sought objectivity to balance his subjectivity while attempting to fuse the various elements of the play to make it work.

They were quiet for a few minutes. She took another cigarette while he held the lighter. For a brief moment he could see how lovely her face was in the bright flame. He looked up. The stars seemed brighter. His emptiness was gone. After finishing the cigarette, she turned and kissed him softly again.

"Thanks for everything," she said handing him his coat before going inside. Soon he followed. Sounds of loud talking made thick with liquor greeted them. The record player blared away. No one had missed them. She melded into the crowd. He felt as if he had entered a different dimension but sensed vague connections. They were well intentioned people. Yet he was certain that he failed in convincing very many of them of the possibilities of theater, even amateur theater. He looked around and sipped his drink. Yes, he thought, I will direct for this group again although he knew the future of serious theater in this area was most doubtful.

Dominic

HIS FATHER HATED HIM. He was sure of that. They shared a name. That was it. As a small boy his father called him "Dommy," which morphed into "Dummy" whenever Dominic did something that displeased his father. Slowly but surely they grew estranged. The distance between them increased even more after his mother died and Dominic went off to the state university. His anger at his father was so great that did not invite his father to witness his graduation.

On a bright sunny June day Dominic received his degree, and the gold bars of a second lieutenant were pinned onto his ROTC uniform. He was newly-minted officer in the United States Army, and soon would be on his way for combat training in Kansas and a few years of active duty somewhere in the world. Surely it would be far away and out of range of the critical voice of his father.

The trip across the country in a slow moving train allowed him time to think of many things. At times unpleasant memories crowded out the more pleasant ones. He remembered playing baseball, a game he loved passionately. It was something that he did well, and he pitched for the varsity team at the university for almost three years. He frowned as he recalled those irritating moments further back in time when he pitched for his high school team. He could hear vividly the rasping voice of his father yelling at him between innings.

"Jesus Christ! . . .didn't I tell you over and over again to pitch the number three and four batters high and inside?. . .my God they hammered the hell out of those slow change-up pitches you tried to fool them with . . . why in hell don't you pay attention? . . . ah shit. . .you'll never amount to anything!"

"I threw what the coaches wanted, Dad!"

"If you listened to me, you'd do lots better. Hell I played minor league ball you know! I know a thing or two about baseball! I wasn't born yesterday, you know! My God, you've hardly listened to me during all of your sixteen years!"

That's how it was during all of his playing days. He heard the same words hurled at him even when he played little league ball. Those words burned into his mind. The harangues continued through high school. His performance was never good enough for his father. But when Dominic reached eighteen he left home and his father for good, and went off to the university on a partial scholarship. That along with his ROTC allowance and his part-time jobs gave him a sense of freedom. Then he could enjoy playing much more because that critical voice was no longer there yelling at him when he took the mound to pitch. He smiled to himself as he recalled his father's reaction when told of his joining the ROTC.

"What in the hell are you going to do that for?" his father asked sarcastically, "You know I'll pay your goddamned way through college! What the hell is wrong with you, 'Dummy'? That ROTC idea is really the most dumb-assed idea you've ever come up with! My God! Suppose another stupid war erupts, and they send you off into some stupid adventure that some ass-hole politicians cooked up!"

Dominic saw his father's face redden with rage but he went on with his rant, "You could get yourself killed or maimed so that you no longer could play ball! If you stayed out of the Army you could make something of yourself, you might even land a pro contract! Haven't you got any damned brains? Didn't I teach you to think better than that? Jesus-key-ryst! Come to your senses, and get out of that Army crap somehow! Wait, I know some people, I'll make some calls."

"No, Dad. I want to do it my way. I want to be on my own."

His father stared at him unbelievingly for several seconds before relenting. Giving in to anything for him was difficult.

"Okay, but don't say I didn't warn you when the shit hits the fan! And it probably will sooner or later!"

Dominic was as stubborn as his father. Neither would budge once they had made up their minds. Dominic stayed in the ROTC, and gradually slipped further away from his father, determined to work his way through college without any help. He even refused the new car offered him, using instead an old clunker of questionable reliability he had picked up for a song. He worked part-time jobs doing anything, finding that preferable to taking any more money from his father.

At Fort Riley he experienced a much more rigorous training and in the process, he learned to be proficient as a platoon leader. Dominic learned how to move and deploy a platoon of riflemen, directing them forward into advantageous positions from where he directed their fire on the large transition range. He learned to drill with more finesse than was experienced at college. Then came a surprise. Life for him and for many others, changed abruptly later that month when the North Korea Army invaded South Korea. That nation had been divided at the 38th Parallel after the World War II, and the United States was committed to aid South Korea. The Army's 24th Corps consisting of the 6th and 7th Divisions had occupied the country but they were withdrawn in 1949, leaving the South vulnerable.

Dominic's training lasted over two months, and then he and the others with him were told they would be shipping out as replacements in combat units fighting in Korea. The North Korean Army had swept over most of the country surrounding a pocket of forces shielding the port of Pusan at the southern tip of the Korean peninsula where American forces brought quickly from Japan attempted to hold them at bay.

During his senior year at the university, Dominic had been recruited by one of the large corporations, and he accepted a position with one of them. His starting date was postponed until he completed his Army duty. He was satisfied with the firm he had chosen because his employment would have taken him to a city a few hundred miles from where his father lived. That was perfect, he thought then, but now the distance between them would be even greater.

Dominic along with many other new officers were now preparing for war, something most of them accepted stoically, considering it merely an annoying interruption in their lives. Several of his fellow officers complained bitterly about their leaving well-paid positions. They sometimes gathered for a 'bull session' at camp and then later aboard the troop transport ship taking them slowly across the Pacific Ocean.

"What the hell are we doing fighting a bunch of gooks off in some God-forsaken country. I can't understand the people in Washington getting us into such a mess."

"Ours not to reason why, ours but to do or . . ."

" . . .oh cut the crap, we're only pawns and cannon fodder!"

Meanwhile Dominic often thought about his father and what he had said as he stared out over the endless ocean. Some of those memories were as irritating as his father's words, which had been right about one thing. But they parted without saying goodbye since Dominic refused to go to the city where his father lived, and his father would not come to see him at the Embarcadero at San Francisco. Now as he watched waves splash against the hull of the ship a wave of regret came over him. During his college days he avoided visiting his father despite the fact that could have, and should have.

His thoughts turned to other things. He remembered Nora, a girl he met just before graduation. For a moment he thought that he could smell her perfume as he leaned against the railing of the well deck looking down at the blue waters. They reminded him of her eyes, bright and eager. He imagined her graceful body lying next to his during those few nights they shared. He neglected writing to her during his stay in Kansas even though he had promised her that he would. In one way he missed her terribly, and in another way he felt it was futile to continue any relationship because his future became clouded by the clouds of a war ahead. Perhaps she had forgotten him by now anyway.

To break the monotony of looking out to an empty horizon, Dominic occasionally went below deck to study field manuals dealing with tactics and nomenclature of weapons his platoon would use. He looked forward to leading men, anticipating that he would be seeing action soon after landing. He was right. After the ship slipped into the bay at Inchon, he boarded a landing craft whose twin diesel engines purred authoritatively while plowing through the water heading to shore.

A regiment of Marines had already landed the day before, and now were followed by units of the Army's 7th Division to which Dominic was assigned. The Marines secured a large perimeter and were moving rapidly east toward Seoul, the South Korean capitol that had been captured by North Korea forces. Some elements moved north toward Kimpo Airport. Marines sought the glory of battle, and they can have it all, Dominic thought. Who wants to get his ass shot so soon after landing? During his unit briefing he and his men learned of their assignment. His regiment was to proceed south to cut off the North Koreans who were hastily retreating from the Pusan perimeter where they had felt total victory was at hand .

The Marines quickly re-captured Seoul while Dominic's unit mopped up fragments of North Korean divisions trying to elude them, many surrendered without a shot being fired. Other regiments joined the Marines and together pushed the remaining North Korean Army back over the 38th Parallel. The front was moving steadily north. Dominic's unit was withdrawn and boarded another transport ship, joining the rest of the division taking them around the east coast of Korea where Marines landed at Wonson. Dominic's units landed further north at a small port called Iwon. Both landings were well above the 38th Parallel.

United Nations Forces from several other countries joined in attacking North Korea, and it appeared the war would soon end. The landing on the east coast met with little resistance. One regiment was assigned to move west to meet up with other UN units. Dominic's regiment was ordered to march north. Two battalions headed for the town of Hyesan on the Yalu River bordering China while a division of ROKs, Republic of South

Korea army units, headed northeast toward the Russian border.

Dominic's Second Battalion was held in reserve at first, but then the commanding general sent it north too. The four platoons of "E" Company, Easy Company, now began the long march heading toward a meeting with the other two battalions.

"What the hell do we need to go way the hell up there for?" asked an irate captain during a briefing held for officers in Dominic's Second Battalion, "Doesn't make a lot of sense since the intelligence people tell us that there is nothing up that way except mountains, some rice paddies, and a couple of fishing villages."

"Look at that map!" said a tall major from Battalion Headquarters Company, "We really ought to fortify a line from Wonson to Pyongyang, that's the narrowest part of the peninsula, and let the gooks up north go to hell!"

"The 'big man' wants to fight the Chinese," offered another staff officer, a major, "He is pissed off because Washington won't let him bomb and strafe across the Yalu into China. He's just another God-damned glory-hound who wants to get China into this war, that's all!"

"Be careful what you say, your career may wind up in the toilet," said a short stocky captain from Fox Company. The West Point officer commanding Howe Company, and Lieutenant Colonel Bowen, the battalion commander said nothing. It was obvious that he and most of the staff officers agreed with the stocky captain and the major.

"Let's hope the Chinese stay put, I want to be home by Christmas," said a captain from George Company. But regardless of their feelings a decision had been made. Soldiers must obey. So the push began to the north with the Second Battalion leading and Dominic's platoon from Easy Company out in front serving as the point unit.

For soldiers on foot it was a slow and tedious march as they plodded their way through the heavy layer of snow that almost obscured the narrow road. Trucks had taken them several miles north until the road grew almost impassable having narrowed into not much more than a wide path. But that was enough for the jeeps, the half-tracked vehicles, and the few tanks that moved along behind the marching soldiers.

The company and the rest of the battalion bivouacked for two nights on their way north.

Living in the field was not comfortable although a supply truck brought warmed C-rations and hot coffee to the men. A tent was erected for the battalion officers to hear reports of the battles raging to the west. Intelligence reports arrived and the trek continued. While a hazy sun followed them the first two days, it eventually disappeared and snow began falling heavily on the third.

Dominic's platoon had three squads of riflemen while the fourth squad rode in a half-track with their mortars, machine guns, and ammunition. From the rear, off in the distance, came the low roar of the tanks from Division, and trucks carrying food and gasoline. Snow fell steadily as they plodded along in the early afternoon. One of the half-track vehicles was sent up ahead of the platoon to crush the thick snow. Half-tracks were three-quarter ton trucks with tank tracks instead of rear wheels, which gave them the ability to plow through difficult terrain. Atop each was an "O" ring to which was mounted a 50-caliber machine gun.

The soldiers of Easy Company marched for over two hours before growing weary, despite the fact that most of them had thrown their field packs onto the half-tracks. Dominic enjoyed the crisp cool air. The white landscape appeared strangely beautiful. Everything seemed peaceful and serene. It lulled him and his men into daydreams of home, but Dominic grew tense when recalling his father's warning about getting caught up in a war. So the old bastard was right, so what? Then he smiled as he realized that so far this mission was like a cakewalk, except for the damned weather.

Easy Company kept going, but there seemed to be no more of those small villages nestled along the road as before. There was nothing ahead, nothing in sight but the high mountains to the left and the lower ones to right. Visibility was poor and an overcast sky blanketed everything in grayness. It grew colder and the snow kept falling. Dominic had an eerie feeling. Everything was going too well. At first the men brushed the snow off repeatedly, but then tired of doing that, they let it pile on them, clinging to them and their weapons slung upside down on their shoulders, giving the column of men a ghost-like appearance. The platoon sergeant suggested sending scouts ahead now that they were beyond signs of life. Dominic told him to send Carston and Rodriguez. Dominic trusted and respected Sergeant Thornton, a draftee who saw combat during World War II, and stayed on in the Regular Army. Thornton had served with the 10th Mountain Division in Italy, earning battle stars and a field citation. He spoke to Dominic after he joined the unit and just before landing at Inchon.

"After I introduce you to the platoon, I want to you keep your mouth shut . . . let me brief them . . .the worst thing you can do is all that flag waving shit that you ninety-day wonders like to do . . . and that don't mean a damn when the fucking shooting starts . . . boys got to become men real quick then . . . they got to learn how to survive . . .suck up all their shit and fight the way they were trained to fight!"

"I'm not from OCS, Sergeant!" Dominic said tersely, "I came from the ROTC."

"I don't give a shit lieutenant; it's the same fucking difference as far as I'm concerned. Most of you college boys think that war is some fucking game . . . something to cheer about like a football game . . . a glory thing! It ain't like that at all. It's mostly confusion . . . lots of noise . . . lots of metal and shit flying around . . . and most of that shit can kill you!"

"Let me tell you something, Sergeant," Dominic tried to interrupt.

"No, let me tell you something!" Thornton's voice rose, "We ain't going to be fighting for Mom, Apple Pie and the goddamned flag! . . .we're going to fight to save our asses from getting killed, we fight for each other . . . we fight to stay alive . . . you got that, lieutenant?"

They stared at each other for several seconds. Dominic felt the heat of Thornton's words and his breath, but turned them over in his mind and realized that Sergeant Thornton was right. War was not like the movies. War was the chaotic hell the Sergeant had described. He had been there. It would not always be like the move south from Inchon had been. There the Marines had taken all the casualties, Thornton pointed out. Dominic smiled, looked him in the eyes, and shook Thornton's hand. He had occasionally in the past met someone with whom there was a powerful unspoken connection, a kind of *simpatico*, understanding that transcended words. That was the basis of relationships. He had felt that with Nora, although with her another dimension had appeared. Now he felt *simpatico* with Thornton.

"Okay, sergeant, you're right . . . I'm with you." Thornton smiled back, realizing that Dominic was different than many of the college-boy wonders he had served with before. He sensed that Dominic was exceptional, and he was seldom wrong in his judgment of fighting men.

The snow was deep in places, and the half-track lurched slowly ahead of them on their torturous path, its engine revving occasionally. Whiffs of exhaust occasionally caught Dominic's attention as the half-track's engine belched an annoying sulfurous odor. He looked up ahead trying to see if Carston and Rodriguez scouting ahead of the platoon were in sight, but they were not. They would signal if anything unusual appeared.

The steadily falling snow was hypnotizing, but the regimental commander, Colonel Barnes, had been clear with his orders. He wanted his regiment to reach the Yalu River as soon as possible. Word had reached him that other units of their sister regiment were already waiting at the Yalu. To him it looked as if the war was winding down, at least in his area of command. That would be fine, thought Dominic, looking forward to finishing his tour of duty in Japan. That would be preferable than living in the field as they were now forced to do. Here there were no showers. No mail, little food. Just cold. Damp. And snow. Lots of it.

The platoon slogged along quietly. The silence was nice. Up ahead of them Carston and Rodriguez were far around a bend in the path when they found themselves facing a squad of strange looking soldiers. They looked menacingly at the Americans. One of them raised his rifle and before he could finish the curse in his throat, Carston was shot in the face. He fell dead. Rodriguez turned and ran several steps before three shots struck him in the back. But as he fell dying onto the snow, he fired his flare gun. Its bright flash hung in the sky for several minutes despite the overcast sky.

Sergeant Thornton saw the light and immediately knew what it meant. Dominic was just about to slip into another daydream when he heard bugles. Not one. Several. And their sounds appeared to be coming from several directions. Then things happened quickly, more quickly than any of those training exercises had prepared them for. Looking to their left, the men of Easy Company saw large numbers of strange looking soldiers racing down the hill toward them firing weapons at them, shouting and waving madly. Some threw grenades whose explosions added to the noise while the bugles screamed endlessly.

Dominic quickly joined Thornton in directing and coordinating the fire of their platoon. Staccato bursts of machine guns fire erupted from everywhere. Some of the enemy soldiers came within a few yards only to be cut down by Easy Company riflemen. Still they hurled grenades before falling dead at the feet of Easy Company soldiers who hurled them back. Then enemy mortar shells dropped everywhere, some even striking their own attacking soldiers.

"Get your asses down! . . . fire at the first line nearest you! God-damn it! . . . keep up fire!" yelled Sergeant Thornton as he and Dominic tried to rally their platoon. Some men cowered in a large ditch to their right. Others took cover behind the half-tracks and also in the ditch. It was too late for several who fell dead or wounded on the pristine snow. Noise and confusion continued. Sergeant Thornton climbed onto one of the half-tracks and pulled the dead soldier slumped over in the "O" ring mount and fired the machine gun point blank into the charging soldiers who kept yelling until they fell dead in heaps not far from the truck.

A soldier in the other half-track chimed in with his machine gun, and the machine gun melody augmented rifle fire from others in Dominic's platoon. The BARs, the Browning Automatic Rifles, joined in with staccato bursts. The two tanks that had been following the column of men roared up from the rear and parked side by side on a low rise facing the oncoming enemy whose soldiers came in droves despite their comrades lying dead ahead of them. The tanks fired cannons point blank at groups of the enemy and sprayed machine gun fire into the enemy. Up along the hillside shells struck rock. Large globs of dirt flew into the air along with odd looking bundles. Those were body parts of dozens of attacking soldiers blown to pieces by cannon fire.

It was later determined that the attackers were part of a large Chinese army that slipped across the Yalu to join the North Koreans. Dominic tried making sense of the surreal scene, which felt like some bad dream in hell. The attackers were dying in large numbers yet they continued to attack. It was as if the waves of soldiers coming at them would never end. They just kept coming and Dominic's platoon kept killing them. Many of his men grew terror stricken, never having experienced such deadly force before. Those that panicked were in the most danger, for the enemy seemed to sense their fear. Many of Dominic's men lay wounded, or dying in the snow, the clean whiteness splattered with red blotches of blood and gore. Time was frozen in the cold air around them. Each moment seemed like an eternity. Yet, Dominic experienced a strange composure while yelling instructions to his men.

Suddenly, he flew through the air. The ground below him pulled away, leaving him suspended in what appeared to him to be like a slow motion movie. In less than a minute his body slammed back to the ground. An enemy mortar shell had exploded nearby; close enough to send his body along with that of two other soldiers flying. Upon landing he automatically began crawling towards his carbine several feet away. Just as he reached it, another soldier fell mortally wounded on the weapon. Dominic rolled the body away, and took up his weapon only to find he could not hold it to his shoulder. A large piece of shrapnel had torn into his shoulder, and as he stood up calling for assistance he was struck in the leg by bullets. He crawled over to several men huddled behind a nearby half-track whose engine was now on fire.

"Watch Sergeant Thornton's tracers!" he yelled, "Fire in the direction they go . . . even if you can't make out anything! Keep up a steady stream of fire! Keep firing, Goddamn it! Keep firing!" They were in a vortex of indescribable destruction. Suddenly it grew quieter. Mortar shells stopped falling around them. It was like someone throwing a switch. Everything was turned off. The call to cease fire could be heard from members of other platoons that had flanked the attackers while still other units of the regiment moved up forcing the attackers to retreat. Meanwhile units of the other regiment moved south from the Yalu River to assist. Wounded men lay all around Dominic as he stared blankly into space. Some of the men moaned loudly, while others just moaned. The shrill voice of one rose above the others.

"Mama! Mama! . . . Oh, God! . . . Help me! . . . God! . . . Jesus! . . . I don't want to die! . . . oh, God! I don't want to die!"

Dominic crawled over to help the man. He was in bad shape, bleeding profusely from stomach wounds. Dominic yelled for a medic who appeared as if by magic as several other cries for help could now be heard.

"Medic! Medic!

"Take care of him, I can manage!" he said as the medic began to examine his shoulder. The medic turned to the wounded soldier next to Dominic, attempting to quell the blood spurting large globs onto the snow. The man had been disemboweled by large pieces of shrapnel, some still protruding from his open stomach. The smells of blood and fecal matter mixed with the urine of the dying soldier.

"This one is really bad!"

The medics hurriedly tried to stop the flow of blood of the wounded using large gauze pads. They moved swiftly, passing over the dead looking for the living.

"Shit . . . oh, shit . . . Goddamn it!" screamed the medic, "Get the God-damned Padre over here on the double!" He yelled over his shoulder at no one in particular. He turned to bandage Dominic's wound, who was surprised to learn that a chaplain was even with their unit. He could feel the sharp pain that he managed to ignore during the fire-fight. Then he felt faint and nauseous.

"You got to save that guy!" he yelled to the medic.

"Too late. . .he's gone!" said the medic. Just then the chaplain bent over the dying soldier.

Dominic heard familiar words, the last rites being chanted over the dead soldier.

"Domine, non sum dingus . . ."

A stray mortar round fell nearby and dirt and rubble flew around them as the sound of the blast almost drowned out the voice of the Chaplin.

". . .erue, Domine, animam ejus, requiescat in pace."

"He's a Protestant!" Dominic screamed.

"He won't mind the prayers, son," said the chaplain quietly.

Dominic remembered Sergeant Thornton's description of the combat he had experienced in Europe.

"Sometimes a battle seems to go on for days, but it may be only a few hours, or just a few fucking minutes," Thornton had said, "Then at other times it seems like it's just a few awful fucking seconds! But the dead and dying are always dead and dying, and the wounded are always wounded! We pick up our asses and move on! The medics pick up the wounded! Grave's registration teams picks up the dead."

How true Dominic thought. How sad and unfortunate it is to die in a war in some God-forsaken country far from home. How pointless and useless is war.

It was almost dark when Dominic was evacuated to the rear, having been carried by litter. When they reached a road, he was loaded into an ambulance with several others and taken on a not very smooth ride to a mobile surgical hospital that had been set up in tents near the town of Iwon. A truck parked nearby was stacked with the bodies of men from his platoon, each wrapped in tarpaulin. What saved the rest of the platoon from being entirely wiped out was the quick response of the other two platoons that quickly outflanked the enemy, catching them in crossfire.

Dominic meant to report his platoon casualties to the company commander, Captain Morrison. But he was weak and lapsed into unconsciousness. Later Captain Morrison was handed thirty-eight dog tags of the soldiers in Dominic's platoon who had fallen. He prepared his report to the Regimental Commander. He studied each dog tag trying to remember the faces of the men who had worn them. He looked sadly at their names, serial numbers, religious preferences, and blood types, the blood that had oozed out of them . . .types "O" or "A" or "AB." He stared at the names of men he knew - PFC Juan Diego Rodriguez - PFC Oliver Joseph Carston - Sergeant James Robert Thornton, and Second Lieutenant Dominic Bailey Callahan. They were gone. From Easy Company, seventy-two wounded were on their way to a hospital ship waiting off the coast.

At the field hospital shrapnel had been removed from his body. He would never again pitch baseball. Scenes and images from the battle blended with hallucinations. There were wounded and dying men around him. His thoughts turned to Nora. He could see her face, smiling at him. He wanted to write and tell her that he was okay. He was sure that he was. He dozed off for awhile. In his dreams he was somewhere else, somewhere where there were no wounded or dying comrades. As he slipped into coma Dominic was pitching baseball somewhere on a warm sunny day. The air was sweet, but then the batter hit a home run, and he expected the manager to walk out and take the ball away from him. But when he looked up he saw it was his father walking toward him and smiling.

"Dommy! Glad you made it, son! You sure scared the hell out of me for a while!"

Eminent Domain

AFTER LIVING IN THE city for many years, Aaron and
Margo Dexter moved to a small town. He found a
teaching position at the university nearby while Margo
taught English and speech at the local high school. They
enjoyed small-town living despite the local inhabitants
who accepted newcomers grudgingly and always with
some degree of suspicion. The locals held a somewhat
narrow view of life, which can be expected from those
who seldom traveled away from their homes except for
a day or two. The inhabitants of the town appeared
to know or care little about history except that some
of them found solace by collecting antiques. Ideas
concerning history and philosophy remained frozen in
the few books about those subjects in the town's library
and were largely ignored.

Aaron and Margo liked their new home
and the town itself although they made few

friends. The natives feared anyone who appeared to be high-brow, equating intellectuality with the snobbery they failed to see in themselves. Some natives voiced the opinion that although Margo was nice, but Aaron must be a communist or something like that. Aaron's beard and habit of riding a bicycle around town made him suspect. There was only one other grown man in town who rode a bicycle regularly, an eccentric sort who was thought to be crazy.

Aaron chose this particular town because it had been the home of one of his students who had been killed during the Korean War. The population of the village was mostly white Anglo-Saxon Protestant and tightly homogenous except for the few dozen families of 'foreigners' living in the northwest corner of town. Despite the fact that most of the immigrants had become naturalized citizens, they were looked down upon for the most part or with calculated indifference. They were considered not much better than the few dozen Negroes living in the same area as the 'foreigners.'

There are always those who have the need to feel superior to others for one reason or another, Aaron surmised. It was likely that their attitude toward those who were different from them was due in part to subconscious feelings of inferiority. That increased their fear of 'others' and was magnified by their egos. It is remarkable that this need for superiority was also found among the 'foreigners' as well, some of whom not only looked down upon the Negroes, but also spoke despairingly of other foreign born including those of their own nationality. Aaron concluded that such feelings clinging to their nature prompted their latent hostility and belligerence making it easier for society to accept war as a solution in dealing with people unlike themselves.

The village was growing and changing but fortunately some things remained the same. In the center of town were two and a half acres of green grass growing under tall elm trees. This green space, surrounded on each side by commercial buildings formed a pleasant oasis. Officially it was called Public Square, but most people referred to it as 'the uptown park. It was 'uptown' because all the streets radiating from it sloped away in each direction.

During morning hours the county courthouse of Romanesque architecture cast its shadow from across the street at the northeast corner. A large fountain crafted from huge stone blocks stood in the center of the park with its water spurting high into the air before splashing down into a small pool. Small colorful fish darted back and forth in their aquatic prison. An old World War howitzer stood sentinel on a concrete pedestal at the Square's northwest corner until replaced by a cannon of more recent vintage to bear a silent obligatory tribute to the glories of war.

Other improvements came during the decade after the war when normal life resumed in the fifties. The green paint had cracked and faded on the old wooden bandstand, which was replaced by a concrete pad providing the community band a place from which to play on warm summer evenings. Aaron enjoyed watching with fascination the town and country folk sitting on wooden benches listening to triumphant march music. Urchins of various sizes and ages ran about squealing with laughter, shouting loudly to each other, ignoring the music and the pleas of their parents to be quiet and stop their running. It was a picturesque setting, almost bucolic, one waiting for an inspired artist to record it on canvas for posterity.

The park endured each of the four seasons with nature's stoic flair. When winter snows blanketed trees and lawn the park took on a wonderfully clean look until the snows in the streets around it melted into a dirty brown mess. But until that occurred, the empty branches covered with 'blossoms' of snow formed a quaint scene for those who bothered to look up as they hurried along sidewalks mostly unaware of the beauty around them.

The goldfish in the fountain were taken to a pond in the cemetery to survive until they could be returned to their uptown venue in spring. During winter pedestrians heading for the courthouse or the library or the school moved rapidly across the park over diagonal sidewalks slicing through the park and its dormant lawn. The wind howled through the trees, occasionally causing clumps of snow to drop onto passersby. Even school children on their way home scurried to avoid the wintry blasts instead of tarrying longer than necessary.

Under nature's rule spring eventually returns. Temperatures moderated as the winds slowed into warm breezes. The trees showed signs of life and soon green leaves re-appeared. A grand canopy took shape above the heads of the children walking and running to and from school. Most were oblivious of the subtle changes occurring around them as seasons changed, yet occasionally a small child, usually a young girl, would pluck a fallen leaf from the ground left over from the previous autumn and carefully press it between the pages of her school book.

The warm weather of spring and summer encouraged the gathering of small groups of people who sat on one of the several metal benches scattered about. What seemed surprising was that not many residents of the community took advantage of the cool comfort afforded by the majestic elms as their branches spread like wings of green angels. Most of those who did sat on the west side facing the stores across the wide avenue where most of the pedestrian activity occurred.

Farmers usually came to town on Saturdays and brought their produce to sell or purchased their needs. They stayed around during the evening for the band concert. On the northwest corner across from the cannon was a three-story hotel with green striped awnings. During warm summer evenings young men gathered near the cannon to gaze up at one of the windows on the third floor where a woman occasionally appeared in various stages of undress. Some waited for hours. The female form always held a great attraction for the eyes and minds of men and boys, even the provincial lads growing up in this town.

The town hall was located across the street to the south and the ground floor held the equipment of a volunteer fire department. When a fire was reported, a factory whistle several blocks away shrieked for ear-piercing minutes while a loud bell rang ominously above the town hall. Volunteer firemen came running from every direction and if driving, parking cars helter-skelter on the street. The big green door opened, and the snout of a red fire-engine appeared, engine revving, siren wailing. Volunteers jumped on before it roared away providing some excitement for those sitting on park benches and those sauntering along uptown.

Aaron usually stood watching with other onlookers until the engine disappeared before sitting on one of the benches. He watched the flow of people going and coming from the stores with amusement. At various paces, life seemed to be movement, even in this slow-paced village. What was surprising was that few people spent time in the park except on Saturday evenings. But during late afternoons and early evenings during weekdays a variety of characters wandered into the square. There was the small band of young men not quite ready to settle into marriage that met in the park, ostensibly seeking something to do. Each sought adventure that was unlikely to appear in the park. They occasionally engaged in roughhousing, name-calling, and the nonsensical palaver laced with occasional vulgarities.

Other more interesting characters made their way to the park almost every evening during summer. A strange pair occupied a bench and puffed with enthusiasm on their cigarettes before going on their way. They were a study in contrasts, one being a huge child-like man, tall and strong as a mule, who worked at loading trucks at a warehouse. It was said that he had killed a man when he was only twelve years old. The other was a small but not so gentle dwarf embittered by his stature. The older kids referred to them as 'Mutt and Jeff.' Mothers would point to "Mutt's' stunted growth and whisper "that's what'll happen to you if you smoke cigarettes!"

Then there was Caleb. He was the one who often rode a bicycle, and often launched into conversations with himself. His voice grew louder by the minute. He spoke angrily about politicians of all stripes damning them for their perfidies. Patents for his inventions were stolen by unscrupulous companies long ago, and perhaps that led to his mental state. Before he was declared a ward by the judge, he lived at an old hotel near the rail depot and after having words with its manager, he devised a way to get even. He dismantled the manager's Model-T Ford outside and stealthily took each part up to his room where it was re-assembled, filling the entire room with automobile. Caleb enjoyed a last laugh but soon after he was evicted.

The most intriguing character for Aaron was a man who spoke little English. Aaron conversed with him using a mixture of French and German most of which the man understood. Eli Ungureanu was a short stocky man with a large head who spoke little English. He was a Displaced Person who came to town shortly after the war. Someone said that he was born in Romania. What English Eli attempted tumbled out coated with a heavy accent, and was not always comprehensible. Some benevolent church group sponsored his entry into the country, and one of its members found a job for Eli as night watchman and handyman. But the church group was disappointed. They had a dinner for him at the church after he arrived in town.

"Oh my! He's not what we expected."

"Where did he come from?"

"I'll bet you that he is one of them communists!"

"Does he even know how to bathe?"

"He's not one of us, that's for sure!"

"We need to get a new service committee!"

"He's definitely not a Methodist."

"Someone said he is Orthodox, whatever that means."

"We shouldn't be so judgmental."

"Would you want him in your home?"

Eli bought a small lot that no one wanted at the edge of town next to the dump. With some help from other parishioners he built what could only be considered a shack. Running water and other utilities were added and Eli was pleased with the results although neighbors were not. But things change. Sitting next to Eli one evening in the park he became aware that something was troubling his foreign friend.

"What's wrong, Eli? Do you want to tell me, sil vous plea?

"They want my home, they want my land!"

"Who, Eli? Tell me."

"Big man, big car come and offer money for my place! He say if I not sell . . . him go to court and get my place anyway! Where me go, tell me where me go?"

"Tell me more about your journey to America."

"The war come. Everybody leave. I walk for days and days weeks and weeks. One day this fellow in uniform tell me where to go. I go. Men give me papers. I sign them. Then I get on boat and come to America. Church group is sponsor, but they don't like me."

"What happened then?"

"One man there find me job. One, two three help me build my house . . . I have home . . . I happy."

"Good for you, Eli!"

"I glad to have one friend . . . you Aaron . . . my friend!"

Meanwhile pressure grew in the town council to have Eli evicted and his shack removed immediately, especially by one of its members whose brother-in-law turned out to be the 'big man in the big car,' a real estate developer He purchased all the land around Eli's shack with plans to build over a hundred new houses. Town council agreed that Eli must sell or be removed by 'Eminent Domain.'

"We got to get that foreigner out of there!"

"Progress cannot be delayed or stopped by one person, the good of the whole community is at stake here."

"I'll contact him one more time and if he fails to listen to reason, I'll file papers to legally take the land in the name of the town and then we can sell it to the developer."

Aaron called friends in the city and soon representatives from a civil rights organization came to defend Eli pro bono. This elated the tired old man.

"How I thank you, Aaron!"

"Don't worry, Eli, they won't win this by a long shot." And Aaron was right, the judge was a firm believer in property rights and ruled in Eli's favor. But certain townsfolk talked with the mayor who was determined to find other ways to remove Eli. And unfortunately Eli provided them with an excuse. Soon he faced the threat of deportation. In some desperate loneliness, which many humans experience, and which Eli lived with constantly, he believed he could find solace by drinking large amounts of whiskey. On several occasions he imbibed enough that made him even less understandable. Sometimes he was seen either wandering aimlessly through the park, or lying on the grass, very drunk. The town fathers took a dim view of such public behavior, and saw their opportunity.

"Listen, Eli!" growled the stern voice of the village mayor one day after Eli was released from the small jail behind the fire department, "If you don't stop your drinking, you will be deported!" He stared intently at the stocky foreigner, waving his finger majestically, "Do you understand me? Now sober up and stay that way, or else you'll find yourself on a slow boat going back to Russia or wherever you came from! Is that clear?" The mayor was certain that Eli would soon get drunk again and that would be the lever to get rid of him for good. That would be all nice and legal.

For several weeks Eli was not to be seen in the park, or anywhere for that matter. Someone said he would show up for work but disappeared quickly after quitting time. When he next walked into the Park he puffed away on his long pipe that resembled a small saxophone as smoke billowed.

He stopped puffing long enough to smile broadly. He greeted everyone, mostly the ever present youth brigade that invaded the park each summer evening, and as he spoke his small mustache jumped up and down happily.

Old Eli was cold stone sober, clean shaven, dressed in a dark suit coat, a cap, baggy blue trousers and heavy work shoes that anchored him. He waved a document enthusiastically, sharing its contents as he went from person to person.

"Me have pay-pers! Me sit-eez-en now! Not dee-port! Not dee-port now! Not dee-port! Ha! Ha!" Eli chuckled loudly between each phrase, his voice squeaking excitedly. His home was safe from the developer and he lived there for several more years. Eli eventually died peacefully in his home. His little house then was razed. The developer had his way. Few attended his funeral. Aaron was there.

Fait accompli

An empty stage. Completely dark. It is totally, and unequivocally dark. It seems like a void; its nothingness is overwhelming, or at least suffocating. After a moment the voice of a small boy off-stage right is heard.

BOY - "Hello."   (*A pause, then softly),* "Is there anybody there?"

A small circle of light appears downstage right and slowly grows into a large circle of light. The boy steps into the light and walks around in it bewildered and confused. He moves into another area upstage center where another circle of light slowly grows into a large one. As he steps into this area, the first area fades out. He moves slowly around as if looking for something. Then downstage left another circle of light appears. He moves into it and the light in the area he left fades. He again looks around bewildered and confused. Then a circle of light downstage center grows and he moves into it as the circle of light downstage left fades. He peers out over the audience, shielding his eyes.

BOY - "Hello. Is anybody there?"

(*There is no answer. A circle of light appears downstage right and he moves into it. A circle of light comes up and grows larger downstage left in which a youth appears who speaks to the boy*).

YOUTH- "It is time for you to go."

BOY- "Is it time already?" *(Short pause)* "But . . . can I just stay for just a little while longer . . . just a few more minutes?"

YOUTH- "Yes, but then you must go." *(Short pause)* "Do you yet know what it is to have regrets?"

BOY- "No, I'm not sure . . . but I would have to do everything the same again, except . . ."

(His voice trails off. He exits slowly off to the right and as he leaves his lighted area fades. The youth walks slowly, repeating the movements and gestures of the boy from one circle of light to another. Each area is lighted as he moves into it while the lighting of the area he left fades. He circles in each area as if looking for something but unable to find. He moves from down left to up center to down right where he peers out

over the audience shielding his
eyes with his hand).

YOUTH- (*Almost fearfully*) "Hello,
is anybody there?"

(*Asmallspotlightappearsdownstage
left and grows into a larger circle of
light. A man steps slowly into it and
speaks to the youth*).

MAN- "It is time for you to go now."

YOUTH- "I know, but can I stay for
a few more minutes?"

MAN- "Yes, but then you will have
to go. Do you have any regrets?"

YOUTH- "A few . . . not many. But
I would do the same things and say
the same things again if I could . . .
if only I could. . ."

(*His voice trails off As he exits slowly
off right and upon leaving his lighted*

area fades. The man now moves slowly around the stage into each area from downstage left to upstage center, and finally downstage right. Each area light fades as he leaves it. He seems confident as he moves, occasionally smiling. Then he reaches the spot from which the youth left the stage downstage right, and he peers out over the audience, shielding his eyes with his hand).

MAN- (*Very loudly*) "Hello, is anybody out there?"

(Light comes up downstage left and into it an old man slowly shuffles using a cane. He nods and speaks to the man).

OLD MAN- "It's time for you to go now."

MAN- "Yes, I know. (*A long pause*) Can I stay for a few more minutes, there's something I wanted to . . .?"

OLD MAN- "Yes, of course." (*Short pause*) "Do you have any regrets?"

MAN- "Yes, I have a few . . . actually, I have many. I would do things differently if I could, but it has been difficult to . . . "

(*His voice trails off. He shrugs his shoulders He looks around moving in a slow, small circle as he does. Then he walks slowly off to the right as the light in his area fades. The Old Man walks slowly to center stage into a spotlight that comes up while the area downstage left fades. He peers out over the audience, shielding his eyes with a hand*).

OLD MAN- "Oh, I know you are out there, and yes, I have many regrets as well." (*Long pause*) "I must go now, but you can stay for a few minutes longer if you like."
(*He turns his back to the audience, and walks slowly upstage and exits into darkness. The spotlight fades slowly as he leaves*).

Gabriel

SOMETHING WAS WRONG. SOMETHING was wrong . . . terribly wrong. Gabe Harrison thought that he was the first to know, and when he first reported it few believed him. But he was persistent, and having farmed for over thirty years he had never seen anything like it. He took great pride in working his own farm for many years. Now he worked for an agribusiness, one of those mammoth food producing industries that evolved from the truck farming of the 1930s.

He knew farming then, and he knew farming now, having watched over dozens of the company's fields for many years throughout cycles of planting, cultivating and harvesting. He did his work as if the crops and the land were his own, supervising a crew of sixty men augmented by a few dozen college kids in the summers, and several dozen immigrant laborers during harvest season.

Several times since his discovery Gabe went out to look at the large acreage expecting something to change. But it didn't and he struggled to understand why. Every inch had been properly seeded using modern farming techniques and the best equipment. Crops failed to appear. Nothing grew. They were long overdue. Yet not a single stalk poked up through the ground anywhere. It was as if the land had swallowed the seeds but denied their germination. Nothing but brown earth greeted Gabe's eyes as he scanned the field in each direction.

"I'll be a son-of-a-bitch!" he exclaimed to no one in particular as he hurled a handful of dirt across the barren field. He knew his job and that of his men was in jeopardy, but more important to him was the feeling that he had somehow failed. That bothered him no end. He was one of the company's field superintendents to discover the crop failure, and the first to inform his company, and the nation about the problem.

What happened next was annoying and perplexing. The company had sent a battery of specialists, several times even, to examine his fields. They would prod and poke but found little fault with anything in the procedures that Gabe and his crew had followed. The experts took endless samples of the soil from various portions of the huge spread. Gabe remained worried but a bit optimistic. Surely they would find out just what in the hell was going on, what was wrong, and why the crop was failing. They would tell him what to do. He would do it. The crops would then grow as before. Everything would be hunky-dory.

As far as Gabe was concerned, there was no logical reason for the crops not growing. But none had. The crew he supervised had done the same things it had done in previous years, working meticulously while following company guidelines based on years of farming experience. There was sufficient rainfall all that spring. Not too much . . . not too little. In fact, the weather had been near perfect. They had even re-planted several sections in each part of the largest fields. Just to be sure. Nothing. Just like those others. And these empty fields were all that Gabe and his crew could show for their efforts.

His frustration grew as he trudged over to the road kicking chunks of dirt as he strode along. He didn't even bother to kick off the loose dirt from his boots as he climbed into his pickup truck and slammed the door behind him. News had come from other company foremen, and Gabe learned that this problem was the same everywhere, not just with his company. It was universal in every part of the country. Same thing. No crops. Nothing. Gabe drove to the building where the company housed its equipment and where he had a small office. Everywhere he looked glum and worried faces greeted him. Even his secretary seemed preoccupied when she brought him a cup of coffee. He filed his report and waited.

A few weeks went by. Nothing had changed. It was in the middle of the morning as Gabe sat in his office with an expression on his face like someone about to be executed. He sipped on yet another cup of coffee. The silence was deafening and he was glad when his secretary spoke to him.

"They're coming soon," she said.

"Who?"

"Another special task force from company headquarters. I just got off the phone. They should be here any minute now."

Gabe gazed up at the large map on the wall of his office. All the company fields were clearly marked. Every one of them was now colored red indicating that crop seeding had failed to grow anything on any of them. Shit, he thought this can't be happening.

"You believe in prayers?" he asked her.

She remained silent as she poured him some fresh coffee, pouting slightly, unable to answer. There was a hint of tears in her eyes as she made an attempt to encourage Gabe before she left the room. The low murmur of voices out in the garage, idle men sitting around playing euchre, was all that filled the silence until the whining sound of a truck motor was heard rolling up the driveway leading to the building.

Gabe thought about cleaning out his office. He expected to be fired on the spot because he could not explain the crop failure. The company was mighty strict and held its people responsible for any, and everything, that happened on their property. It was a huge corporation, not some fly-by-night deal. It was a no-nonsense operation from start to finish involving bio-chemical research, botanical plant research, managed planting, methodical cultivation followed by irrigation, harvesting, shipping, food processing, packaging, and national distribution. This building and the fields around it were duplicated around the country in dozens of locations, and each was now reporting the same inability to grow crops despite repeated attempts.

The special task force from headquarters consisted of five men. They were specialists in every phase of agriculture: chemistry, agronomy, and botany. Each knew how seed developed into beans and grain and vegetables and finally into money. Profit and loss . . . the bottom line. They came into Gabe's office solemnly, not with the swagger they previously displayed during several visits. Everything seemed wrong. This should not be happening. Losing one crop was critical. Losing all of them was unbelievable, a financial disaster of epic proportions. One of them spoke.

"It's the god-damndest thing, Gabe!" he said as he slumped into a vacant chair next to Gabe's desk. "We've been to a dozen other fields. Each of them looks exactly like yours here. Frankly all of us are stumped! We've taken soil samples everywhere, had them analyzed every possible which-way there is. Shit, all the soils test just fine . . . balanced, and fertile. Some even exceeded all known standards. There is nothing wrong with the god-damned soil! There is nothing wrong with the seed! We've double checked all the various fertilizers and planting methods used; they've only been improved over the years. But still we can't grow anything . . . not a goddamned thing!"

Gabe was relieved. He began to feel that way when the reports of other foremen experiencing the same difficulties in growing anything filtered in. I'm not to blame he thought, somewhat relieved but still disturbed. Yet there was nothing to be excited about, he was in the same pickle as before only now he could share it with others. Misery surely loved company.

"I've brought in the samples you requested. I left them in the truck . . . I'll get 'em for you."

"Yeah, we might as well run them through the mill. But I have little hope that we'll find anything different, anything that will show us what the hell is wrong." Gabe was happy to hear that at least it was 'our problem,' not just his problem.

"You know we even replanted parts of sixteen fields over at Charlie Turner's spread. Same thing. No results. It's the damnedest thing I've ever seen," then after a pause, "don't know what the hell to make of it"

Gabe was relieved that no mention was made of firing him or anybody else. But his relief would be of short duration. He sent one of the crew to his truck to retrieve the dozen soil samples he had collected that morning. After examining records kept at Gabe's office, the five specialists took the soil samples and left, each looking as glum and forlorn as if they had been attending a funeral. Gabe felt hopeless. There was nothing he could do but wait. The company sure couldn't afford to keep paying wages to his idle crew, or him for that matter, not to mention all the other hundreds of their employees scattered around the country.

It didn't take long for the bad news to arrive. Within a few days everyone but a small maintenance crew at each of the company's locations was furloughed. In a matter of days, experts from all corporations involved with agriculture met in a series of meetings in Washington, D.C. There were formal hearings in both houses of Congress. There were also hearings held at various locations throughout the country. Solemn faced men and women representing all the huge agribusiness corporations in America filed into large conference rooms at the Department of Agriculture. Several congressmen and senators sat at the head table along with three members of the cabinet including the Secretary of Agriculture who was the first to speak.

"Gentlemen, what on earth is happening to our food supply? What is going on out there in the breadbasket of America? The companies represented here are responsible for over two-thirds of the crops of this nation. What do I tell the President? What can he report to the nation? Please tell me something good now!"

"We are completely baffled, Mister Secretary," responded an executive from Gabe's company. "We've tried everything under the sun . . . we've examined every acre of soil. We've tested and tested. There seems to be no answer. Every soil sample shows the ground to be fertile."

Senator Walsh rose to speak.

"By God you've got to do something!" he shouted, "Evangelistic ministers are on television telling listeners that this crop failure is due to the sins of the people of this country for allowing all the rampant pornography and atheism. According to them it's God's will, they say, and it is His punishment for the sins of the people! Especially because of all the abortions, all the sex on TV and in the movies and all the deviant sexuality due to the rise of homosexuality! Talk show hosts are making jokes at our expense! They got everybody praying up a storm! Some on the Hill are saying that this must be an act of terrorism, or that the communists are doing this to us! Why can't any of you tell us just what the hell is going on? Can any of you find any evidence so that we can defend ourselves against these claims?" His voice shook at times and finally he dropped into his chair.

No one spoke until an assistant under-secretary of agriculture reported that the problem of crop failure was occurring only in our country. All foreign countries reported usual crop activity, and none reported any fields failing to grow after planting. But surely the rest of the world could not send much of their food supply to this country. And surely the people of those nations could not be entirely free of sin.

"Let's cut out all this talk of sin. Remember how many times the president has asked God to bless our country? Could he have been wrong? Would God treat our most favored nation thusly? I think not. There must be some foreign power messing with us. This has got to be sabotage by some of those damned terrorists wanting to make trouble!" said another lawmaker.

A man in back rose to his feet. He was the CEO of another huge agribusiness combine, one even larger than the one that Gabe worked for. He ignored the previous speaker's remarks.

"There has got to be some rational explanation for all of this. Things like this can't happen without reason. Where in hell are all these experts that we have hired? We pay them good money, why can't they tell us something besides sitting there shaking their heads like a bunch of loons?"

Then a respected scientist from the university was asked to speak. His manner was direct and objective.

"Look, insults and innuendoes aren't going to help. We in the scientific community have studied this problem for weeks, ever since it was brought to our attention. And we continue to struggle with it. Maybe it's a result of Global Warming. Certainly the atmosphere has been affected by the presence and growth of humanity. Harsh words do nothing to help. . ." his voice trailed off and as he sat down, tears streaming down his face.

"Maybe those preachers are right, maybe God is punishing us," said a man in the front row, "maybe it's the Apocalypse after all." Someone in the back row murmured, "Bullshit!" Then Gabe's CEO spoke again. He corroborated what the scientists had reported, but now he asked Gabe to come forward. It was a moment that Gabe dreaded, having to speak before all these very smart people. He had barely made it through high school before starting his own farm. He made his way slowly to the podium and stood awkwardly for a few moments gathering his thoughts. He stared out over the assembled group, coughed nervously, and then with his careful manner of speaking he made a startling revelation.

"I took a truck-load of soil from one of my unproductive fields, and dumped it in my back yard. My wife then proceeded to grow every kind of vegetable you can imagine without any difficulty. It's the craziest thing! My wife can grow tomatoes the size of bull's nuts. They are large and sweet . . . the tomatoes, not the bulls nuts . . .but out in our company fields we can't grow weeds! Something's gone wrong somehow! But I don't know what or how! And to top it off, all my neighbors up and down my street are planting in their backyard and everyone of them is growing stuff right and left. It just doesn't make any sense." Gabe's voice trailed off as he looked around the room and then awkwardly left the podium and returned to his seat.

"My people," said his company CEO, "have checked around and found that everywhere backyard gardens are flourishing and producing! Only the fields under mass production and those of the few family farms left in the business are failing to yield any crops. It's absolutely mystifying, totally unexplainable."

Senator Craig exemplified those in positions of power who assume that they are superior in knowledge having grown accustomed to have been treated as though only they were wise and noble. They were certain that only they held the necessary answers to every problem, political or moral. But now he too displayed his apprehensions.

"The food supply is reaching a critical stage! Many of our markets are totally out of fresh vegetables and cereals! Cattle are dying for lack of feed. Terrorism is growing in our towns. Armed men are beginning to roam the streets in certain areas taking produce from neighborhood gardens at gunpoint. Are we going to continue having these pointless meetings while the country is one the verge of anarchy and terror? What can we do?

We are relying on you scientists to lead the way now!" Then another speaker from the Department of Agriculture spoke.

"I am alarmed. I recently visited a farm nearby and as I stood there the most startling thing occurred. Newly planted crop was just beginning to appear, but while I stood there every stalk slowly vanished into the earth. The ground simply swallowed every bit of that planting. I think Mother Nature is trying to send us a message of some kind!"

"And what might that be?" asked another exasperated senator who obviously thought that the speaker was insane.

"The message may be that we should stop polluting the earth and the air that surrounds it. It is possible that if some signs of activity along the lines of definite reduction in pollution, it might alleviate the situation and allow crops to grow again. The idea of climate change is not conjecture! It is a scientific theory that is sustained by factual observations and very conservative calculations!"

A loud murmur echoed around the room followed by a strange disquieting silence for several minutes. Then another man, a professor from the State University was called upon to speak. Professor Sebastian Gabriel had been commissioned by the Department to bring his expertise to bear on the problem, or at least to provide some explanation. Gabriel was a specialist in agronomy and noted for level headed thinking. He sipped from a glass of water, hesitating for a moment before speaking and looking out warily at the people wanting answers. He spoke quietly and earnestly.

"There is something called the Gaia hypothesis that states that the earth is a self-regulating organism." He waited for his words to sink in, "It posits an alternative to the idea of a mechanical world. The earth is like a giant being of its own. Some conjecture that the Gaia is, or has, some kind of knowledge, a higher level of consciousness, and a definite purpose beyond our knowledge. Perhaps it is speaking to us through its soil, refusing to allow crop growth to gain our attention as to what is happening throughout the realm of nature."

Professor Gabriel sat down. It was very still for a moment and then the audience stirred restlessly. Everyone seemed to be talking at once, a mixture of amazed and angry voices erupted from every corner of the room.

"Where did you get this guy? And just what in the hell does all that crap he just said mean?" asked one of the irate senators. "We cannot listen to a crackpot like that?"

"The professor is spouting absolute nonsense!" interrupted another colleague certain that none of them believed such a theory. Those in the room began to look at one another incredulously, but it grew very quiet. The idea was sinking in. What if it were true? A big if! Was nature the enemy now?

The meeting adjourned. The food shortage increased dramatically. Rationing of food began. Importation of food increased. Prices soared. The wealthy could afford to pay anything. Poorer people grew weak and frail. Some were unable to eat the meager relief provided. An economic depression cascaded across the entire nation and grew as profusely as the crops did not.

Many workers in agribusiness lost their jobs followed soon by thousands of food processors, and thousands more working in food distribution systems. The democratic civilization began its slide into oblivion while its leaders postured and blamed each other. Some even blamed God. Most of them were reluctant to face reality. But Gaia had spoken.

Hubris

IT WAS VERY DIFFICULT for those sitting in the classroom to pay much attention to Aaron Dexter's lecture. Spring had arrived with its usual grand flourish as nature bathed the campus in warm sunlight, caressing it with warm southwesterly breezes. The lecture seemed to drone on for most of the students, and some glanced wistfully out through the open windows at a small group of students lounging on the lawn just outside Gadsden Hall with envy, wishing they could join them.

Those inside listened to the lecture half-heartedly, their minds far away lounging in areas far removed from his words. Most were induced into a melancholy feeling by the tonic of the spring air that occasionally wafted into the building. The bucolic serenity of the outdoors beckoned, contrasting sharply with the information coming at them no matter how diligently the words were framed and how well they were being said.

"...and as we know, most of this century has been caught up in wars that extended around the globe, causing great sufferings for large numbers of people . . . and many of these wars grew out of the fears transmitted to the people . . . now we have a senator destroying reputations by calling government employees and others communists, implying that they are traitors to this country in some way and jeopardizing our freedom . . ."

Dexter paused. Looking over the twenty-one pairs of eyes in his class, he saw that several pair was gazing out the window while others appeared to be almost somnambulistic. Although he understood the nature of young people, he himself having been one long ago, he felt the need to regain their attention and teach what he knew best. He was quite aware that his words were passing over their heads like a muted benediction.

"...and as I was saying . . . it may be better if we have a change of pace." No one seemed to be aware when he stopped talking and stood a few moments contemplating his next move as if it were a chess game. He decided that a question might arouse the students from their slumbers, or at least draw the attention of some. His mind concluded that it was time for a bit of free-for-all, a method he occasionally employed. He would engineer a give and take allowing students to digress and speak to each other about whatever issues might capture their fancy.

"What was the significance of the British Trade Labor Movement . . . what were the consequences that followed, and how was this event a major turning point in history?. . .do you see any relevance to current events in any way, and if so, explain as best you can."

That brought a few students who had been slouching in their seats to a more upright position and even those gazing out at the heavenly scene outside looked up with surprise.

"Didn't we cover all of that during our last six-week period?" asked one of those not looking out the window, "I thought we did, I mean, gosh, that's old stuff, isn't it?"

"Yeah," said someone else, "We went over that twice as I recall, so why do we need to rehash that now?"

"Of course it is old stuff . . .my God the whole course it old stuff! After all, you must know, this course is called history for some reason . . . and yes we covered it before . . . hell, we covered everything before, but review is part of your task . . . it is essential and useful and while some of you may not find it as intriguing as what is transpiring out there on the lawn, you need to be clear on what the ramifications of the labor movement were and they were, indeed, substantial. . . "

He paused before continuing and noticed that most of the twenty-one students were now paying attention. ". . . for they affected the entire structure of successive societies lumbering out of the industrial revolution . . .I do hope that you remember something about that as well. . .why, there may even be a question or three about both of these subjects on your final examination, which I am sure, will count mightily for your final grades!"

"Holy smokes, he's right, exam week is mighty close!" said one of the students who had been dozing and now seemed very much alert.

"Yes, and some of you will graduate and not have the privilege of having to listen to any more of my lectures, so you may wish to take advantage of them while you have the chance to absorb some of their penetrating ideas instead of gazing dreamily out the window!"

The first volunteer to respond was Nora, a female honor student who was considered one of the brightest students in all of her classes. Her answer almost took the form of a lecture as she rambled on while classmates listened with little enthusiasm. One student was doodling lazy spirals in his open notebook. Another was drawing what appeared to be football plays with lines sprouting out in every direction. A third sitting near the open window followed the movement of a bird making a lazy loop around a nearby tree before settling on a branch. Others sat listening to Nora as she concluded.

" . . . there is no doubt that the Trade Labor Unions were influenced by the Communists and perhaps they were even linked directly with a part of the Bolshevik adventure, and I might add that the . . ."

"Goddammit!" interjected Aaron who practically leaped out of his chair, "God almighty damn! What the hell are you saying? Is that the best you can do?" He frowned but aware that if the question hadn't gotten their attention, his outburst would.

"What do you mean?" asked Nora.

"It is extremely upsetting to have an honor student come up with such a bunch of nonsense . . . your remarks are nothing but hog-wash . . . way off base to a straight-forward question . . . and just what in hell does Communism have to do with the Trade Labor Movement? My God, Nora, you of all people certainly should know better . . . because there you sit wearing the Phi Beta Kappa key as one of our honor students! How can you come out with such absolute drivel?"

He stared at her angrily, but it was an act and she was part of it, "What is the world coming to?" He looked around the room at the others, "Can one of you other dolts wake up and enlighten her with a rational answer more to the point?" After a short pause, Harry always eager to display what he considered to be his mighty intellect, rose to her aid.

"What she probably meant to say was that the labor Movement had socialistic tendencies, a trend that was developing in much of Europe at the time, just as it was doing here in the United States."

"Listen," said Martin, another student who now wanted to prove a point, "There never was much of a socialistic movement in this country . . . it had little effect or no effect except to scare a bunch of people . . . oh, sure there were some radical left wingers in New York . . . but it is clear that our system is the best form of government . . . it is of the people, by the people, and for the people! A free market system that is the envy of the world, we gave the world a great democracy, supplying the greater good for the greater number and ensuring freedom for all."

"Okay, Mister Lincoln . . . but you need to know that the greater good for the greater number was first uttered by a socialist! But pray, tell us more," coaxed Aaron. Martin was momentarily stunned but then Tobin decided to take the plunge.

"Marty forgets that we the people stole much of the land in this country from Native American Indian Tribes who were living here long before 'we the people' came storming over from Europe and shoved them aside. And what happened to the idea of all men are created equal . . . and they have rights to life liberty and the pursuit of happiness?"

"Okay 'Jefferson,' men are created equal, but the Indians weren't humans. They were just a bunch of savages . . . they were heathens . . . not really people in the sense that we know of as people," Martin countered. The professor was aware that the students were digressing but he enjoyed their sarcastic exchanges and at least they were now awake.

"There were over a million Native Americans in fourteen ninety-two when Columbus stumbled onto the Western Hemisphere and by nineteen hundred there were only a quarter of a million of them left. That's not progress . . . that's genocide!

"So what?" was all that Martin mumbled.

"The Indians were forced to endure relocation, disease, and genocide. Their subsistence patterns were broken resulting in malnutrition and starvation despite the many treaties our government signed, promising them a share of the land. In the end most of these treaties were forgotten or ignored"

"For example?"

"For example in the Treaty of Fort Laramie in eighteen sixty-eight the Sioux tribes were promised the Black Hills in what is now South

Dakota but when gold was discovered there, they were forced out much like the Cherokee were made to leave Georgia and later Oklahoma when oil was found. Let's face the truth . . . Native Americans were badly treated."

"How do you know all this stuff, it's not in the text we are required to read and study?"

"One of my neighbors when I was growing up spoke of his Indian blood and told me some of this. . .the rest I got by doing a little research over in the library for another course . . .but more importantly we need to know that history was watered down in grade-school and we need to know the truth." Then another classmate chimed in.

"Yeah, Martin, and I suppose that little trick of slavery that existed until eighteen-sixty-five was a neat idea, huh, providing plantation owners cheap labor while counting each male slave as three-fifths of a person so the owner could vote to maintain his luxurious life-style!" Aaron watched quietly as Jim tried to support Martin's position.

"The slaves were savages too . . . and it's certain that they were better off here than they had they stayed in Africa . . . after all, most of those Negroes were sold to Portuguese and Spanish traders by other Negroes, and as for the Indians, they were given territory for the land they ceded to the government, so they haven't got anything to complain about!"

"Jim both you and Martin are full of crap, and you both know it . . .ceded land my eye! Practically every treaty our esteemed government made with Indian tribes was broken, their land was taken by force of . . . the United States Cavalry. . . and they were shunted around from corner to corner of this country before being shoved onto reservations, made to live in an alien way, a way destroying their culture and meanwhile slaves in the South had no chance to develop . . .unprepared for emancipation after which segregation became just another kind of slavery keeping them in poverty and ignorance . . .and like the Indians, they too, were denied education . . . often left to starve . . . subject to disease and death."

"Well, neither the Indians nor the slaves built this nation. It was the pioneers and those who settled the west . . ."

"Oh, bull hockey!" It was Harry speaking excitedly now, "It was the thousands and thousands of immigrants from Europe working in mines, factories, steel mills, and on farms who did all the real work building this country and the society that followed."

Martin was eager to change the subject. "Well, our professor thinks that John L. Lewis was some kind of a God . . . it was the labor unions that made all the problems in this country with their socialistic and anti-commerce attitudes." Tobin was angry now, but Nora rose to redeem herself.

"I found the reference to the British labor movement on page four ninety-five. It began with the Christian Socialists, a man called John Mac Murray, a Scottish philosopher who held the left of center idea that opposed raw individualism and wanted to promote solidarity without collectivization . . . in other words, he championed a united society working through cooperation."

"Fat chance that could work!" That was Harry again, now with a touch of anger discernable in his voice as he read loudly from the text, "In the eighteen hundreds during the first part of the Industrial Revolution, the quality of life went up for some and down for others while the effort to eliminate child labor was opposed. There were no safety regulations, and little relief was supplied for those who could not afford food, and then when relief was given . . . wages were lowered."

"That doesn't give people the right to interfere with the growth of capitalism or the accumulation of wealth! They just delayed the prosperity that was around the corner. In other words they were standing in the way of progress!" said Martin.

"If you had to work in one of those damned mines or mills under the conditions that were present, you too might think John L. Lewis was god! Guys like Carnegie, Rockefeller, and Ford displayed little interest in the well-being of their workers while building their fortunes."

"But all three became great philanthropists and built libraries and created foundations supporting lots of good things."

The professor interjected, "We must get back to where all this began with our country and its place in the order of things as history has demonstrated." He paused for a moment, "Are the truths mentioned in the Declaration self-evident? If not, why not, and why haven't these ideals been applied to all segments of society, and just as importantly, where is conscience to be found? Can there be such a thing as a collective conscience?

Can those who benefited from past actions share the guilt which made such benefits possible?

He paused again, "Suppose for a minute things had been different at the outset. Imagine that the economy of cotton growers had been successful without slavery, could the economic engines that created wealth have operated in a way that rewarded the labor of those needed for its success?"

Nora spoke again, "Cheap labor, especially during those formative years was required for successful operation of enterprises like growing cotton, or mining, or manufacturing ... cheap labor has always been made available in some form, and it still is . . .but slavery was permitted and plantations of the south needed it to operate because Native Americans wouldn't work for white people . . .cotton growing didn't stop, but later much of the back-breaking work was done by machines instead. Some of the freed slaves joined poor white people as sharecroppers eking out a miserable existence, requiring their children to work along with them in order to survive. That kept them from school, keeping them in ignorance and poverty for generations."

"What about the Indians?

"The American Dream in Red?"

"Yes . . . why not?"

"There was that quaint idea of Manifest Destiny. White people considered themselves Christian, therefore better, and did not accept or tolerate Indian customs. The early settlers were religious people after all and for them Indians were heathens worshipping strange idols. So, we stole the land from them! Maybe now we are being punished for the follies of the past, for the sins of the past, by having racism, ignorance and poverty hang on indefinitely."

"So what's the answer?" asked Martin, "It can't be socialism, that's just like communism!"

"But there is a difference between them. You need to learn more about that . . .both were responses to miserable conditions of workers during the Industrial Revolution. Communism advocated revolution by force and abolition of capital and private property while Socialism saw that reform could be accomplished by parliamentary and evolutionary methods."

"Yes, in lit class we read George Bernard Shaw was a socialist who felt that mankind was too dumb to create a real working socialist system, unable to find ways to cooperate for the common good."

"Our government is too socialistic!" Martin protested. He managed to find label or slogan to fit his argument. He seldom listened to what others said, especially when Tobin answered

"But you benefited by public education, a form of socialism, and now you benefit from a socialist higher education. This university was built by tax dollars and your education is being subsidized by social taxation!"

Somewhere a bell rang. Class was over. The students sat upright, awakened by vigorous argument. They seemed reluctant to leave. Professor Dexter smiled and dismissed them with a wave of his hand. The twenty-one rose and began filing out of the room, some still arguing all the way down the hall as they headed for their next class somewhere. Dexter was pleased. He harbored the theory that education had to be more than the accumulation of information, lists and dates of events, even their relationships. The object of education included not only all of that, but most importantly the ability to think.

Ineluctable

THE ROOM WAS DARK. There were no lights or windows. There was no heat. The man wrapped himself in a torn blanket that had been thrown at him after he was rudely shoved into the room. Then he curled up in a corner trying to capture whatever body heat he could retain. The room was devoid of furniture. There was nothing else in the room with the man wrapped in the blanket except a bucket in another corner of the room. That was there to contain whatever urine and feces the man would pass. The man did not know how long he had been in the room. Time had disappeared along with the light.

When first brought to this place he was taken to an office somewhere in the building. He vaguely recalled a man of some authority sitting behind a desk. Questions were asked for which he had no answers, but he remembered that the man behind the desk was somehow familiar resembling someone that he must have known somewhere sometime. But who? Where? When? Everything blurred in his mind. Thoughts floated through his head but none of them connected with anything.

He could not remember his name at first. He had a feeling of nothingness, of not really even existing. He reached for his wallet, but it was no longer in his pocket. But then the clothing he was wearing now seemed strange as well. The trousers had no pockets anyway, but the reason he wanted his wallet was to look for some identification, to find anything that might bear his name. That would be a clue. And where was he? Why was he here? Had he been here more than a day? It seemed as if he had been there all of his life.

It was good deal later that he remembered his name and that occurred only after several agonizing hours when suddenly it appeared in his mind. Yes, that's it he thought, almost shouting it aloud. I am Adam. My name is Adam. He paused. But Adam what? What is my last name? More anxious moments passed as he tried to wipe away the dull shadows moving about his brain. Then it came. Finally it came. His surname was Brystik.

He was Adam Brystik. Gradually other memories entered his consciousness. He remembered that he had eaten several times, and each time the light from the corridor almost blinded him when the door was opened just long enough time to allow a strange person to place cup of water with a piece of bread resting on top of it just inside the door.

Adam once tried to bolt out when the door was opened, but another larger person grabbed him quickly, and forcefully threw him back into the cell with such force that Adam fell in a heap against the opposite wall. His sides and shoulder hurt. That must have been the first time the water and bread were delivered. He did not try to bolt past into the light again but lay still and closed his eyes as much as he could, trying to blot out the strong feeling growing in the pit of his stomach. This must be a dream, a bad dream, he thought. Yet he was in a prison of some kind. But why? What had he done to deserve this?

Adam thought for quite a while before he remembered how it all began. He had been walking down the street minding his own business. Four men approached him. They were all large men, huge. One of them spoke to him and before he knew it, the other three surrounded him. They bound and gagged him, and threw him into the back seat of a car parked nearby with its motor running. There must be some mistake, Adam thought. They have arrested the wrong man. But no one ever said that he was under arrest. He knew that he had not committed any crime of any sort during his entire life. His only brush with the law was a few parking tickets. Oh, yes, there were also a few speeding tickets, but no felonious action of any kind to blot his spotless record.

Adam spent hours wondering if anyone knew of his plight. His situation. Or circumstances. And time? Where was it? And truly, what was time? How much had gone by? And did anyone know or care of his whereabouts? Did anyone care about him at all? But then why should they? He seldom thought of others. He remained strangely aloof all during his life. He was a loner. As a matter of fact, he felt superior to most people, treating almost everyone but his superiors with studied indifference. He was aware that he had a slight fear of others, occasionally he felt in awe of others, things he reluctantly admitted to himself. His manner had been to question what others could do for him with little thought as to how he might be of use or serve them in any way. He lived alone. An older woman, a testy old woman who dressed like a refugee, came to clean his apartment occasionally. She did her work and left without speaking to him, merely grabbing the bills he held out to pay her. He never had visitors. His family lived in another city, and he preferred it that way. In all likelihood, they did as well. He felt nothing for them. They reciprocated.

Gradually he became numbed by his solitary confinement to the dark cell, and in a strange way grew accustomed to it. It became sort of a home to him. It was familiar. Despicable it may be, but still a home. It was similar to something else that he was not totally aware of until now, a numbness of his life in general. He had gone through the motions of living but in reality, Adam had merely existed . . . like some strange particle floating through space and time, an ameba, or a germ, just enlarged chunks of bacteria glued together and encased in meat.

Sitting alone for God knows how long he grew to realize that he had hardly lived at all. He had been like a parasite living machine-like without thought or feeling. And now this had happened to him. Why? What was ahead for him in this prison where he now found himself? Surely it must be a prison. Days went by, one by one. Maybe it was a month. Maybe it was several months. Years even. Who knew? But Adam became oblivious of the passing time and cared less about it. His numbness grew to the point where he no longer even cared that he was confined.

One day, the door opened and stayed open for much longer than usual. Adam did not recognize the people standing in the doorway. They motioned for him to go with them, and a deep penetrating fear overwhelmed him. He felt the fear permeate into every fiber of his being. Cowering in the corner wrapped in his blanket, he refused to leave the cell when ordered and mumbled incoherently as the men beckoned to him. He had grown attached to his blanket. The two men again asked him kindly, almost affectionately he thought, to accompany them. Were they going to execute him, Adam wondered? Yes they must be planning to kill him. That seemed a likely possibility.

The light from the bare bulbs illuminating the corridor hurt his eyes. He shut them while being lead, one of his captors on each side of him. They were practically holding him up, half dragging him along. They took him into another room after passing through a long hallway. The room Adam found himself in had one table with three chairs around it. A harsh bare light bulb hung above one of the chairs, the one into which Adam was thrust. He was left alone for a short time. What he did not know at the time was that he had spent almost nine months in that other room existing in solitary confinement. He was confused then, and he was confused now as two men, two different men, entered the room and sat in the empty chairs their faces hardly visible peering at his from the shadows.

"Who are you working for?" asked one. He had a deep voice that frightened Adam at first. The other man spoke then, more calmly and with a voice that seemed less harsh.

"Why are you here?"

Adam did not know what to say and when he began to answer his voice emerged with a stuttering hoarseness because he had hardly spoken since his incarceration. His voice was gone.

"What is your assignment?"

"You brought me here!" he managed to stutter, "You tell me why! Yes. . .I want to know why?"

"We'll ask the questions! All you need to do is answer them!" said one of them. Then the other spoke.

"Who do you work for?" He waited but Adam had no answers. He tried to think of what to say. He had forgotten where he had been working, or even if he had been employed. Nothing appeared in his mind but the thought that he must be guilty of some terrible crime that he must have forgotten. Then a light appeared in his head. He knew he had worked for the government in some secret work, which now he had forgotten.

"We know there are others," growled that other deep voice in the shadows.

"What are their names?" asked the other man who was now smoking a cigarette, "Tell us their names!"

"I don't know what you mean, I don't know what to say," responded Adam who grew more apprehensive by the minute, "I don't know who you are asking about. I don't know anyone!" He blurted out as his anxiety grew along with the pitch of his voice. Then he remembered an instruction he had been given long ago in another place to give only your name and serial number when captured. But now in his stubbornness he decided not to tell them anything if he could help it.

"You have been named," said the deep voice.

"We know that you belong to an organization that is known to be linked to terrorists threatening our nation. We know a great deal about you, don't think we don't," said the other man.

The interrogation was repeated for several days. Maybe it was several weeks. Things grew worse each time. During the second interrogation and from then on, he was strapped to the chair. His ankles were shackled. The lighted cigarette the one man was always smoking was placed against his bare arm several times during the questioning. The pain was accompanied by the putrid smell of burning skin. Fortunately there was a positive thing about the questioning. Adam passed out several times and found himself in a blissful sleep. That and the fact that he had been moved to another room down the hall. It had a cot and a toilet as well as a small table. And he was given a small meal each day. A tepid broth and a piece of meat joined his daily bread and water.

But then things also grew uglier. The questions were always the same each time, but the torture increased. Adam collapsed in his chair several times during each interrogation. Electric shock had been added to the repertory, usually contacts fastened to his private parts. Adam no longer could remember who was asking the questions. His mind went blank and he could not answer any question. There seemed to be different men each day, and each of them enjoyed applying the torture. There was word for that he thought. It finally came to him: *Schadenfreude.* Yes, that was it. On more than one occasion one of the large men slapped him sharply across the face to arouse him after passing out. He often thought about faking it but never had to because he actually fainted during most of the interrogations.

On other occasions he was strapped to an inclined table of sorts with his feet elevated above the level of his head which was held in place by pads fastened to the table. Water was dropped into his nostrils until he began suffocating. It was stopped periodically only to be repeated later. These sessions continued intermittently for some time until finally one day the men did not come for him in his room. Adam was shocked to find he had spent an entire day all alone, or what had seemed like an entire day. His meal that evening was of a better quality. There was more food. Having lost track of time Adam wondered how long he had been detained and what day it was. What year it was. He forgot what city where he had been living. What startled him was that he no longer seemed to care.

Then one day his original clothing was returned to him, neatly cleaned and pressed. They now looked strange and unfamiliar to him. He didn't know why but he cried as he put them on. What is happening he thought? What are they going to do to me now? Perhaps there is a firing squad outside and he was going to be shot! He was frightened when escorted into an oak-paneled office on some other floor of the building. An imposing figure sat behind an enormous desk talking to someone on the telephone. It was the man who had talked with him when he first came here, but now he looked somewhat different than Adam remembered.

Adam was motioned into a seat opposite the desk and sat with his head bowed looking down at the floor. The two men who brought him left the room without a word. Finally the familiar looking man put down the phone.

"So, how has your stay in our friendly little hotel been for you, eh?" He was very pleasant and cordial. He looked at some papers in a thick file for several minutes saying nothing. He lighted a cigarette and turned to speak to Adam.

"We regret any inconvenience that you may have experienced in your short stay with us," he said, "And after you sign these papers you are free to go."

"Wh . . . what are they?"

"This is a waver. That one states that you have been treated well, and that one is a receipt for your personal effects which have been returned to you this morning."

The three papers were handed to him along with a pen. Adam stared at the papers. His vision blurred, and he was unable to read the words on them. He sat looking around furtively like a trapped animal. What are these papers? Were they some kind of confession? He began to tremble, but suddenly remembered that he was in his own apparel again. He had eaten better. He relaxed somewhat. He took the pen and slowly and awkwardly scrawled his signature across the bottom of each of the papers. Two men appeared and escorted him out of the building.

Adam walked slowly down the street and looked back over his shoulder apprehensively several times. He had walked several blocks before remembering something that he had seen in that oak-paneled office. It caused him to stop. His eyes widened and he caught his breath. A dreadful moan erupted somewhere inside of him, but it did not leave his lips. He gasped as he remembered the nameplate on the desk of the man who granted his freedom. The name he saw in bold type on that desk was unmistakable, he remembered it clearly now . . . it was . . . ADAM BRYSTIK.

Jurisprudence

AT THREE IN THE morning on a humid summer day, a state highway patrolman followed a car because the officer felt that it was 'suspicious.' It was an older car, puffing blue exhaust smoke reflecting in the headlights of the patrol car. The patrolman may simply have been bored with the routine of his work and was prompted by his imagination. The older car pulled over to the side of the road and stopped responding to the flashing lights of the cruiser. The officer cautiously approached the car and stood at the rear of the open driver's window. The driver and his companion were laughing at some joke between themselves. The officer was not amused.

The driver of the car identified himself as Billy Joe Draper and when questioned, informed the officer that he and his companion were on their way home after attending a party. The trooper ordered the man from the car and proceeded to give him a sobriety test, which revealed that Draper was indeed sober as he had said. His companion, Linda Mason sat quietly in the car while a local policeman drove up as back-up and parked behind both cars. That policeman had suspicions also and thought 'something was up.' The car was headed in a direction opposite of what the driver had declared to be his destination. Draper and Mason offered no objections to having the vehicle searched by the officers.

The search revealed nothing but to be certain, the local officer radioed for a third officer to bring a drug sniffing dog to join them. The dog sniffed around inside and outside the car for several minutes, his handler following him closely. Again, nothing suspicious was found except a white pill in the woman's left jacket pocket. The trooper and the two policemen left her sitting in the car while they stood in front of the trooper's cruiser using its headlights as they looked through a 'drug book' attempting to identify the pill. After leafing through several pages they found something.

"Damn! It's oxycodone," exclaimed one of them, "sometimes they call it perkadan, probably some brand name." The female was ordered out of the car and questioned.

"What's this pill for?"

"It's for a bad toothache I had."

"Why haven't you taken it then?"

"Saving it as to when the pain gets real bad."

"Where'd you get it?"

"Tommy Grimes gave it to me," one of the officers grunted signaling disbelief as the two others nodded in assent.

"What's the big deal?" asked the woman.

"This is a controlled substance. That's the big deal and it's illegal to have it without a prescription. Do you have a prescription for this medicine?"

"No, I don't have no prescription for it!" she responded testily, "I told you before that Tommy Grimes gave it to me at the party we were at after I told him I had a real bad toothache, and I expected it to come back sometime and then I'd take the damned pill. What's wrong with that?"

She was abruptly handcuffed and taken by the patrolman to his station where her statement was taken. She was told to read it and then sign it. She did as instructed. Then she was released. Two months later, a grand jury at the county courthouse indicted her with felony possession of a controlled substance. A date for Linda Mason's trial was set. It would be over a year since the 'traffic stop' was made on that humid summer night.

An assistant prosecutor represented the state during the trial, and it appeared to potential jurors that the young lady was headed for a stay in the state penitentiary. Her court appointed attorney was a shrunken little old man who appeared inept compared to the robust young prosecutor. However, the proceedings would show that looks could be very deceiving.

An entire morning was spent on jury selection. The portly judge looked bored, obviously needing more exercise than rolling a ball-point pen between his fingers, which he did all throughout the questioning of potential jurors. He did occasionally throw a question at one of the prospective jurors to show that he was still paying attention to the proceedings. Finally after each lawyer used up their peremptory challenges, the last juror was hastily selected. He was asked just one question, the same question by both the prosecutor and the defense lawyer.

"Can you render a true and honest verdict based only upon the facts of the case as shall be disclosed?" The last juror responded in the affirmative to both. He was an older man who shuffled slowly to sit in seat number twelve where he rose to take the oath before sitting down.

The patrolman was the first prosecution witness. He repeated the routine facts of the traffic stop, pausing occasionally to refer to his copy of the arrest report. He told of the subsequent finding and identification of the pill. In response to questions about some details of the arrest by the defense, he stumbled a few times saying that he could not remember. That was surprising since he had ample time to review the circumstances of the arrest, the subsequent interrogation of the defendant, and the statement taken from her following the arrest. The policeman took the stand next but could add nothing to the trooper's testimony except his suspicions. Both were certain of the defendant's guilt and stated so when asked while the defense counsel sat quietly raising no objections.

That afternoon the defendant took the stand in her own defense. She said she had no idea what the pill was when it had been given to her except that she had been told that it would stop the pain of her abscessed tooth, nor that she knew at the time that it was illegal for her to have it. Defense counsel pointed out that neither the patrolman or the policeman reported whether or not Tommy Grimes had been questioned regarding the pill, and whether or not he had legal prescription for it, and if he had indeed given it to the defendant. The prosecutor tried to get her to contradict herself and the circumstances of her having the pill in her possession.

"You knew what it was, didn't you?" He paused allowing the jury to absorb his words. "You knew that the pill was a drug of some kind didn't you? . . . didn't you say it was 'perk-a-something?'" He looked at her incredulously.

"Objection, your honor!" interrupted the defense counsel, "She stated quite clearly already that she had heard the officers refer to the pill by the name perkidan, or some such thing. That's how she got the idea to call it perk-a-something!"

The objection was sustained. Closing arguments followed. The prosecutor was matter of fact in his approach to the case and he too seemed willing to send the woman to prison. He made a forceful presentation. It was logical and factual.

The old defense counsel slowly rose and walked over and leaned against the jury railing. He began talking very softly to the jurors; his measured arguments refuted each of the prosecutor's points one by one. His voice slowly grew louder and more forceful with each sentence, and when he ended his closing arguments it had risen to a crescendo. He had carefully defined the case for the innocence of his client, repeating each salient point. The twelve jurors and one alternative were led into the jury room to deliberate.

The thirteen, nine men and four women took their places sitting around a large circular oaken table. The four women sat next to each other. Several jurors poured themselves cups of coffee from the counter nearby. Before leaving the room, the bailiff spoke.

"You need to select one of you to be foreman, and that person will be responsible to control your discussion, conduct the voting, and have you each sign the verdict sheet."

"Can we leave to go to rest rooms?" asked a juror.

"No, there are rest rooms over there through the two doors behind you. You've already found the coffee and doughnuts that are here for you. Meanwhile I will order lunch for each of you so please write down what you want from this menu I will pass around." Jurors selected and wrote down their lunch preferences and the bailiff left with them.

There was an awkward silence as the thirteen strangers looked at one another for a few moments. During the trial they sat in two rows facing the court, and now were looking at each other for the first time. Some stared at the others quizzically. Some wore the bored expression of casual indifference. None of them seemed to know what to say or do. Except for one man. That was the older man, Juror Number Twelve, who sat erect in his chair while the others slumped or slouched in theirs. The man was a professor of some kind somebody said. Another thought that he was doctor while a third was certain that he was a minister. As one juror said later, "It was his eyes; he had a way of looking at you, like he could look right through you or something!"

"You talk a lot, you should be foreman," said one of the jury members after the others stopped babbling. There was another long pause while everyone turned to look at Juror Number Twelve again. No one else seemed willing to take on the responsibility so the 'professor' became the foreman and he started the group on their deliberations. At first it was somewhat disorderly with a few rambling on with several talking at the same time. Occasionally there was an embarrassing silence.

"They got her dead to rights!"

"Yeah, she had the pill on her, didn't she?

"What do you mean? She didn't know what it was."

"Makes no difference, ignorance of the law is no excuse!"

"They got her sure dead to rights!"

"And what were those two doing out there at that time of the night, I'd like to know? They must have been up to something!"

"Yeah, something no good," offered one of the women.

"They were at some party, probably boozing and doping all night long like those kind of people always do!"

"She had a child when she was sixteen, why wasn't she at home taking care of it?" said another woman juror.

"Aw, hell, that kid has to be eighteen by now and can take care of himself," Responded a man across the table.

"Still, a mother belongs at home."

"Let's leave the morality question for church and the preachers. This is a court of law," said the foreman. He cut short some overlapping conversations that sprang up again. Everyone grew quiet as he outlined the case as it was presented to them in the court room from start to closing arguments. He did that without notes, relying instead on his memory which seemed to be complete. He had not missed anything. He stopped and looked around at the jurors and then took a white pill from his pocket and placed it in the center of the big round table.

"Are you ready to convict the defendant because of one pill," he asked, pointing to it. The jurors looked at one another and sat stiffly in silence.

It was then that the bailiff returned accompanied by a sheriff's deputy carrying large satchels containing lunch for each of the jurors. The deputy passed out the various luncheon orders after calling out the items as he pulled them one by one from the satchels.

"Here's the burger on rye. Who's got the sandwich with mustard and pickle?" A few went to the bathroom while others passed the food around the table. Soon everyone was eating and chatting about things other than the trial of Linda Mason. After they finished eating, the foreman asked them to resume their deliberations.

"But she couldn't deny her having the pill and the police proved that it was a controlled substance, something forbidden by law in this state, right? She's guilty alright! No doubt about it."

"She didn't know what it was, that's all," said another.

"Yeah, but if she did know what it was, didn't she have plenty of time to ditch it while the trooper was giving the driver the sobriety test!"

"Or she could have thrown it away while the drug doggie was sniffing around outside the car!"

"Or while the cops stood around waiting for the drug dog to show up and sniff things out!"

"Sure, she could have swallowed the damned thing easily."

"Twice over!"

"Amen to that!"

"Don't matter, she broke the law and she must pay the penalty, that's the only right thing for us to do."

"Wait a minute, cops are always eager to stick somebody in the slammer and some of them, not all of them, but some of them get carried away. I don't trust them like I used to when I was a kid. They are a different lot today, you know!"

"That's for sure; they just aren't honest as they used to be"

"Yeah, look at our politicians?"

"Too bad we can't put them on trial for something."

"Let's get back to the case."

"Okay, you're right; we got to get this thing over with."

"She must have known what it was."

The same arguments were repeated but perhaps they were not heard when they were first presented. Words flew back and forth across the table and it appeared that several jury members felt that the defendant was guilty. The foreman decided it was time for him to speak again.

"Some of you may be taking prescription drugs, or have taken some in the past. I have. Stop and think for a moment. Did any of them have a warning saying not to share them with anybody? Doctors tell us not to do that, but that admonition is often ignored. And consider this, the police did not say whether or not they verified if it came from a legal prescription, and remember, they did not even say that they talked with the man who had given her the pill."

"No, by God! They didn't say a damned thing about that. They must not have bothered to talk with him at all."

"And why didn't the cop who brought the drug sniffing dog take the stand? It's clear that the dog found nothing, but still the cops both said they detected the smell of marijuana in the car."

"You can't convict on smells, can you?"

"Maybe you can in this state!"

Each juror had an opportunity to speak and the foreman asked the three members of the panel who had not spoken if they wished to say anything for or against the defendant. They did not, but one of them asked to read again the instructions given to them by the judge. While he was doing that the room grew quiet again. After he finished reading the instructions, the foreman stood up and looked over the jurors.

"Take a moment to think this over carefully," he paused before continuing, "Is there anyone here who believes that the defendant knowingly and willingly had in her possession a controlled substance contrary to law?"

"I think she's guilty as charged." But he was the only one who believed that the state had proved its case.

"Are you sure?" asked the foreman.

The man looked puzzled for a moment but when he realized he was the only one voting guilty, he quickly changed his mind.

"I won't get in the way, I'll vote with the rest of you."

The foreman signed the not guilty sheet and passed it around for the others to sign. Then they informed the bailiff. Someone belched softly. Others finished sipping their coffee or soft drink. One went to the rest-room. The foreman picked up the white 'pill' still in the middle of the table.

"It's just a mint," he said. After the prosecutor, the trooper, the defense counsel and the defendant were back in the court room, the jury filed in with their verdict.

Kolya

IT WAS AN ADVENTURE. At least that's the way it began for the small boy. Initially he enjoyed being outdoors all the time, sleeping during the day time and running at night. For his parents and the others it was more like a trauma or a bad dream. They had left their homes and most of their possessions and now fled for their lives. In the group were over thirty men, women, and several children who walked and sometimes ran along in a southerly direction. They moved only during the night in order to avoid an army that was retreating to the west and whose path they were certain to cross occasionally.

The boy ran cheerfully along at first, his left hand held in the right hand of his father. The boy's right hand was held by the left hand of his mother. However running along in semi-darkness soon grew to be less than the fun it was at first. Stubble from some of the fields they hurriedly passed through pricked his legs despite the long woolen stockings his mother made him wear. On the third day it rained steadily all night adding to their misery. Their clothing was soaked through and they desperately sought any kind of shelter. There was little of that in the open country they chose to move through, and they always skirted towns and villages in their path. They might be seen and reported.

After a few days the fun had vanished completely and along with it any sense of adventure experienced those first days and nights. The boy began absorbing some of the fear that his parents and the others felt. After several days during one of their stops, the members of the group held a conference and decided their chances would be better by dividing into smaller groups. The boy along with his parents and two other couples waited until the others were gone for over an hour before resuming their trek. Soon the small supply of food they brought with them was exhausted. The men began stealing vegetables from gardens behind some of the farmhouses near their path being careful not to take too many lest their presence be discovered. They must not be seen. They must keep moving.

During the day they stayed in woods out of sight, sleeping under brush or in an isolated corner of a field, hiding until dark. The need for food led them to grow desperate at times. Then one of the men would approach and ask for food at any nearby farmhouse while the others remained hidden. Some farmers and their families they encountered were friendly. Some were hostile, fearing they would be discovered harboring or aiding enemies. That was punishable by death. Surely these vagabonds must be enemies of some kind to be running away.

That's how it seemed to the boy when terror struck the small band several times during their flight. Once several army tanks rumbled along a road next to which they were huddling in bushes. The tanks were later followed by trucks filled with soldiers. A few times they saw groups of weary soldiers troop dejectedly along as they hid near another road waiting to cross.

"Be still, Kolya!" his father would whisper, "don't make a sound, they are passing close by!" The seven of them lay hidden on the ground, afraid to breathe as the ragged column marched along not too far from where they lay hidden. They could not tell whose army the soldiers belonged to, and they stayed hidden until night came again and the soldiers were far out of sight.

"Remember Kolya, if anything should happen to me you will need to care for your mother. You must do that, son. Will you remember that? Can I count on you?" The boy nodded and wondered what could possibly happen to his father. Soon afterward he fell asleep. A few hours later he awoke very hungry. But it was time to move on. Soon after crossing yet another road and disappearing into another wooded area, they found a clear stream where they satisfied their thirst.

The couple leading them picked up the pace and soon Kolya was running again. When they became exhausted they slowed to a walk, but the others were now far ahead of them. They were prisoners of time, losing track of the days that seemed to join one another endlessly in a pattern of hunger, thirst, and weariness. It seemed to the boy that they would be running and walking forever. When those thoughts occurred to him, he felt a pang of homesickness remembering the house where they had lived before starting on this wearisome journey. Still, at times, during those nights when there was moonlight it was almost pleasant walking across fields and fording streams while tiny stars blinked serenely down at them. Kolya wanted to look up at them but his father and mother insisted that he watch where he was stepping.

"We cannot stop and look at the stars now, we must continue, we must keep moving!"

"But where are we going?"

"We'll know when we get there son, then we'll know."

"I'm hungry!"

"Yes, I know, we all are," said his mother. She searched through her knapsack, "Here take this apple that I have . . . eat it and you will feel better." They walked several miles more that night before stopping to rest. Most of the little band was still sleeping as dusk came upon them one evening when Kolya woke and spoke again. He knew only a few words and now stood pointing down the path they were intending to follow.

"Man!" He spoke loudly without fear thinking that what he was seeing must be someone like them, someone running away as they were doing. His father looked up and was going to shush his son when he also saw the man and froze in his tracks. It was a soldier standing thirty feet away with a rifle at his hip pointed right at them. The others rose. A look of terror came over their sad faces.

"Halt!" yelled the soldier to them even though they made no attempt to move toward him. Then he spoke softly as if he too did not wish to be seen or heard.

"Who are you? Where are you going?" asked the motionless man with the rifle.

"We are merely poor farmers just trying to get out of the way of the war that is coming at us again!" said Kolya's father, "We mean no harm to anyone . . . please let us pass in peace!"

"So you are deserters too, eh!" the soldier laughed.

"Deserters? No, just poor farmers who want to . . ."

"I know I know . . . I heard you." The soldier laughed again and pulled the rifle over his solder using its sling. "I too am trying to get out of the way of the war. . . I have seen enough of it, too much of it. My home is not too far from here and that's where I am going now."

"You won't tell anyone about us being here?"

"No, but you are wise in leaving quickly now for the ones coming from the east will treat you even worse than we did." With that he stepped by them and started walking away. Suddenly he turned and returned with a small bundle.

"Here is some food for you, I'll be home in a few hours and won't need it, but I can see that you do." He handled the bundle to one of the men and soon disappeared, marching off toward the west. The small group was hungry and quickly ate the bread and the two cans of sardines before resuming their flight.

Several days passed. They walked at night and slept as well as they could during the day always fearing that they would be seen and discovered. One morning as they began to look for places to sleep Kolya discovered another word to say.

"Home!" He stood pointing down into a small valley at the center of which stood a barn. Not far from it stood a small farmhouse.

"Be quiet, Kolya!" His father turned and the men talked softly among themselves for a minute. It was decided that one of them would approach the house to ask for food and water. The one chosen quickly left and the rest of them watched as the man disappeared into the woods. Soon he reappeared below them looking around furtively. They saw him move behind the barn and walk slowly toward the house. A few minutes later he entered the house and soon after he came out and waved to them before running up the hill stopping only to yell at them.

"The house is empty!" The others quickly joined him. "The people who lived there must have gone away. Maybe they are like us . . . running for their lives. Maybe the war is getting nearer than we thought! Either way there is food there, and perhaps we can spend the night because it looks like another storm is brewing," he said pointing up at dark clouds that were slowly coming their way. If staying indoors for a while were possible it seemed like a good idea. Kolya's father had a fever and was not feeling well. For the past few hours he had been walking with great difficulty using a long branch he had fashioned into a cane. He had stifled coughs several times during the previous night. The little group descended warily and eventually went into the house where they found dry food and plenty of water. Then the ominous but now pleasant sound of rain splattered on the roof above them. But now they were warm comfortably sleeping in beds, which was a welcome luxury. Kolya's father grew worse during that night and could hardly sleep. His fever increased and he coughed a great deal. The next day the group gathered to move on, but he was not able to walk.

"Go on without me! I will just slow you down! You must continue . . . you must get over the border as soon as you can! Do not let me hinder you . . . you must continue!"

"Yes," said his wife to the others, "Go, I will stay with him. Kolya and I will stay with him." She motioned the others, "You go on!" But the rest of the group was divided over staying or moving on. Each of them wanted to and had expected to stay in the house for a few days anyway. So they all decided to stay for just one more night. That night Kolya's father died. They all shared the sorrow because Kolya's father had been their friend for many years. Yet they knew that they must leave soon. They wrapped him in blankets. Shovels were found in the barn, and they dug a grave on the hillside above the house. Kolya's mother stood sobbing softly as her husband was placed into the ground. One of the other men said a prayer that Kolya had never heard before. A large stone was placed over the brown earth.

It seemed strange to Kolya walking along without his father nearby, but the group moved on, determined to reach safety. They watched more soldiers and trucks and tanks pass them every day while hoping that the war would soon end. Several days later Kolya found another word to say, "Lake!" The others jumped up from their sleep and everyone stared out over the large body of water that greeted their eyes.

"No, Koyla, it is a river!" said one of the men.

"And how can we get over to the other side?"

"We must steal a boat somewhere!"

"And get caught and sent to a camp? Oh, no that's not for me! I would rather drown trying to swim over instead of taking a chance on getting caught stealing anything!"

"The river is too wide to swim over . . ."

"We should at least follow it to a place where it is not so wide before we try doing that."

"Let us find a bridge to cross over."

"Oh, sure that's a bright idea but remember that bridges are always right in or near a town.

Do you wish to be caught now that we have been walking for weeks avoiding towns! Do you want to spend what time you have left in a camp?"

The people grew quiet as the one now leading them walked on. They followed him and the river for a few miles until they saw the bridge arching across the water. And there was a town there too where a few people were seen moving about. From their hiding place a few of the small band spent most of the day watching people coming and going over the bridge while the rest of them slept.

That night after it grew very dark one of their more courageous members slowly made his way into the town. His plan was to find the shortest route to the bridge and return with that information. He did so, and then he lead them quietly and carefully as they made their way along a narrow street through the town, crossing the bridge and reaching the other side where they again disappeared into the night.

They had walked on for several more days before realizing that there were no more soldiers to be seen anywhere. They arrived at a very wide road over which a long stream of people moved in what appeared to be a river of misery. Some of the people carried satchels. Other people pushed carts piled with their belongings. They looked like walking dead, all poorly dressed, filling the roadway and moving slowly along. As products of war, displaced persons by the thousands, homeless with little hope, they trudged westward not knowing where they were going and some not really caring anymore.

They were just glad not to hear the blasts of cannons and mortars around them. The scene was peaceful in a strange but pathetic way. Kolya's small group joined the procession hoping it would lead somewhere for they too had no idea where or in what country they now were. A few of the refugees shared meager foodstuffs with them. After following the roadway for three days a truck with a large red cross painted on its side came along and stopped every few hundred yards dispensing bread and canned food to the sad looking people.

Eventually the long column reached a city of some size where all of them were herded onto trains that took them to a port near an ocean. There, after a security check made by serious looking men wearing strange uniforms, the refugees boarded a rusty steamship. Kolya was confused and bewildered by all of this. He had no idea where he was or where they were going, but at least they no longer had to hide from soldiers and no longer had to run across fields filled with stubble and sleep in ditches during the night. And they were given food. But on the fourth day of the voyage Kolya's mother took sick. She reminded Kolya of his father. She had the same tired look in her eyes. But she did not suffer as much because she died soon after.

Kolya watched as her body weighed down in a canvas sack slipped into the placid blue ocean waters of the Mediterranean. A strange man who must have been a priest said a few prayers that Kolya could not understand but he knew were different from the prayers said over his father. Fortunately for Kolya, his mother had told others aboard the ship Kolya's name or else no one would have known who he was.

Kolya spent the rest of the trip looking mournfully back toward the place where his mother's body had sunk into the vast expanse of water that seemed endless to him. He also thought forlornly of the land where his father was buried in a field in some country unknown to him. He grew sullen, oblivious to the others when they grew excited when the ship passed something the others called Gibraltar before pushing on into the Atlantic Ocean. Kolya remained moody and lethargic even days later when the ship passed by something called the Statue of Liberty. Soon after the ship unburdened itself of its human cargo. Once ashore, Kolya stood silently with the other people as they waited to begin a new life.

Kolya was placed in a series of foster homes in New Jersey. Most of them were in small towns. No one seemed to want the small boy despite the fact that he was very polite, extremely shy and unassuming. He was so quiet that he dissolved into the background of any group he was part of, where no one noticed his presence. He liked it that way, and in a strange way he felt secure when alone. And he did not mind having an unusual name. Later in one of the schools he attended, when others made fun of his name, Kolya simply joined them in laughter. He too, thought his name sounded funny and did not mind their jibes even when their intention was to be derisive.

Kolya learned a new language, and forgot the few words he had learned in his native tongue. He always felt a strange dread that followed him from the time that he and his parents began running through the countryside trying to escape from something he knew nothing about. His thoughts were often those of sorrow, but his anxiety diminished even though he felt isolated, especially when surrounded by laughing children at school.

He studied hard because there was nothing else to do, and because he was promised that sooner or later a nice man and woman would adopt him. He would then live in one place. That would be nice he thought. That did not happen soon enough. The years passed. When Kolya was in his third year of high school he discovered that his feeling of dread was absent during history class, but strangely it returned after he left the classroom.

His history teacher was Mr. Zackary Keegan, who spoke of history as though he had actually been witness to events that happened years ago. He spoke as if he had been there while recounting details of the lives of Alexander the Great, Caesar, and Napoleon. This excited Kolya. One day Mr. Keegan asked him to stay after class.

"Nicholas, I have a book that I want you to have . . . it may be useful . . . as a matter of fact, I am certain that it will be most helpful for you to understand your being."

"Thank you, Mr. Keegan!"

"I know that you are puzzled by your origins." Then he explained that he had compiled a history of the war that raged for several years and he told Kolya about his parents and their village. Mr. Keegan knew exactly when and where Kolya was born and he told Kolya many things about the little village he had left, the one from which he ran through endless fields at night while tired and hungry. Kolya hurried home. He became absorbed in reading the book about his father's country. It was his homeland, too. After supper that evening, he lay on the smooth lawn in the back yard, looking up at the stars enjoying a strange tranquility that seemed to come over him. It was as if the world and all the stars above were standing still . . . waiting for him. Everything was as it was meant to be. Kolya understood that now. Life was whole. He was at one with the universe. He was sure of that now.

Legacy

THEY PLAYED CHECKERS ALL morning as they had done several times before. It was a bright sunny day and when looking out the window they glanced at the splendid lawn of Shady Green Acres. Like a verdant carpet it rolled off into the distance until arriving at the row of tall poplar trees forming a natural boundary for the grounds. Perhaps it was this scene that prompted Bailey to talk about his childhood. Some older people often can see their earlier days with greater clarity upon reaching a certain age.

"You know, I often think about my old man and my growing up when I sit alone in my room. Lots of memories come flooding back," said Bailey wistfully.

"Yes, one thing about this place is that we've got lots of time to think about lots of things,"

Aaron smiled as he moved a piece over next to the 'king' row. Looking up, he too paused for a moment to look out at the broad lawn surrounded by tall trees.

"My old man was a taskmaster if there ever was one," Bailey went on, "He used to beat the hell out of me if he caught me lying or anything like that."

"You mean that he abused you?"

"No, no. . .nothing like that. He was strict. . . that was all, he had a sense of value that he wanted to instill in me, and I think that he eventually succeeded to some degree."

"Nothing wrong with that I suppose."

"Well, sure, that was okay but I did something terrible with what he taught me. . .I changed it to suit my own view of life and as a result of that, I treated my own son so badly that he and I became estranged. . .we grew apart."

"And he was the boy who was killed in the war in Korea, right, the one who was commissioned in ROTC?"

"Yeah. . .my greatest regret is that I never had the chance to make it up to him. . . God knows I wanted to! But it was too late by the time I woke up. . ." His voice trailed off into silence.

They played on for a few more minutes. The only sound came from the round checkers sliding over the board or one being slapped with a 'crown' upon reaching its goal. Bailey sighed and leaned back for a moment and looked across to Aaron.

"Tell me about your boyhood, were you always the smartest kid in the class? Did you decide early on to become a teacher?"

"No, at the outset I was extremely timid . . . awkward . . . tall and gawky. All kinds of strange fears both real and imagined occupied my mind relentlessly . . . my parents each had successful careers of their own and were much too involved with them to pay much attention to me."

"That piss you off and make you study harder, huh?"

"Not exactly. But my shyness was almost debilitating and grew more intense, ruling me for many years. I moved as cautiously through puberty as I did through my own home. One of my constant fears was intruding upon the space and time of others, especially adults, thinking I was unable to offer them anything or contribute to their conversation. I often ran home to seek permission when playmates invited me into their homes, certain that I should not enter their homes without approval."

"Wow, that doesn't sound like much of a joyful childhood."

"Eventually I grew belligerent toward everything and indifferent to school. My parents finally dispatched me off to a private school where I made a startling discovery. I found that on occasion I truly enjoyed learning and even grew to like some studies immensely while throwing myself into athletics with reckless abandon. The success that followed surprised me and my confidence and my cunning increased allowing me to mask my feelings while my ego, fortified by accolades earned on the playing field, reinforced my self-esteem."

"Sounds like you made real progress at that school, what happened next?"

"Sure I made progress . . . becoming an insufferable young man, more obnoxious than intelligent, more impulsive than wise, and decidedly foolish. It was when returning home at the ripe old age of fifteen I learned that I had been adopted. That astonishing information puzzled me more than it upset me. It was shortly after that revelation that my father lost one of his fortunes on the stock market. That distressed my mother terribly, enough so that she took to drinking more than social grace condoned."

"And here I thought that you were the perfect man!" said Bailey. Aaron merely smiled and continued.

"Fortunately a trust fund had been set up for my education in advance, permitting me to attend the college of my choice, but I developed a subtle anger at father and mother for having kept the secret of my origin from me. This anger simmered underneath my outward civility toward them. But that was due to the false pride magnified by my ego, providing me with a *raison d'etre*. It took years for me to realize that, but I finally did and reconciled with them before they died."

"That's something I was not able to do with my son, but go on, your story is fascinating."

"At college I was considered a boy genius on campus where my scholastic achievements far exceeded my athletic abilities. After graduating I found a niche in academic life earning several advanced degrees and was awarded a chair at the university, one of the youngest ever to be so honored. During this time I passed through a series of beliefs, wending my way through them before deciding that I was an atheist, reasoning that ancient man created god out of necessity to explain and justify his existence.

"That explains a lot about your thinking. But you must have moved on beyond that ... haven't you?"

"I met a strange but pleasant man while sitting on a park bench who led me to envision wider perspectives offering me an awareness of a path that might permit me to become what I was meant to be. I began looking inwardly as intently as I had been looking outwardly, amazed to find that I really knew very little about myself despite all that education. Believing that I knew everything to believing that I knew nothing came as a sobering shock. From that point on there was a noticeable change in my attitudes, rash elements of my personality tempered. I shifted into a comfortable agnosticism deciding it was a more appropriate fit matching my ambivalence."

"Then you got married and lived happily ever after, right?"

"Yes, I met Margo at a workshop out in the country at some kind of retreat where I solidified my understanding of life. Margo observed the change in me and became my lifelong companion.

The rest is history. But we were unable to have children and that's when Nora came into the picture. Remembering the pain I endured upon learning that I was an adopted child, I made sure that Nora was informed quite early about hers."

"Where is she now, do you get to see her often?"

"She lives in the city," Aaron said, "That reminds me, I've been meaning to telephone her . . . she gave me this new-fangled device and told me to keep in touch." He pulled a cell-phone from his jacket pocket and showed it to Bailey who had grown tired and decided to go to his room to take a nap. Aaron chose to take a walk. Using his cane he shuffled out beyond the stone patio and wandered onto the green lawn. He sauntered past some hedges next to which stood a beautiful rose bush. He leaned over sniffing one of the large red flowers. He remembered that his mother loved roses and there had been an oasis of flowers near their house. Aaron the boy enjoyed smelling their fragrance and viewing the flowers in the bright sunshine.

The sun must have been the first god, he mused. What was astonishing was how powerful belief grew, perhaps even before language developed. It became encrusted in the people's minds as he imagined civilization's origins where reading and writing were not as yet discovered. Perhaps that is why early beliefs grew and magnified over thousands of years, partially due to the suggestibility of those early beings.

On the plus side there was the receptivity of the mind to learning and understanding leading to the expansion of knowledge. That prompted innovation, everything fueled by necessity. Yet everything is matter, he thought. Everything is energy, and with the imagination of a few, civilization progressed along with the supernatural power. Aaron then turned to something more immediate.

"Call me anytime if you need anything, Daddy. Will you promise to do that for me?" she had written in the note accompanying the package it came in. Aaron fumbled with the small numbers on the phone until he managed to push the required buttons. Somewhere miles away another phone rang and a pleasant voice answered.

"Hello!"

"Nora?"

"Yes."

"It's your father calling, my dear!"

"Dad, are you alright ... what do you need?"

"Everything's fine Nora, I just wanted to tell you something that you need to know."

"What is it, Aaron?"

"This is to let you know that I am now a bona fide resident of Shady Green Acres, or as one of my acquaintances here called me, just another 'inmate.' Last month I finally gave up the apartment, and my friend and colleague, Sebastian kindly drove me up here."

"Are you sure you are okay? You know that you are always welcome to come live with us here in the city."

"I know that and I appreciate the offer, but this place is just fine. It's quite nice here, and you are not to worry about me. That's the message. At least here there is always someone around to remind me to take those pills. The last time I forgot caused the emergency people a good deal of consternation, and it embarrassed me no end."

"I'll catch the next flight out and be there tomorrow!"

"No, no! I'll be fine. You stay put!"

"Are you sure?"

"Yes, I am positive."

"Well, it's good to hear your voice and you do sound as chipper as ever! What is it like there?"

"I made a few friends already and play checkers regularly with one fellow who had been an accountant of some kind."

"Checkers! Did you give up on chess and bridge?"

"No, I just found how interesting the game of checkers can be and how my mind had been closed off to it, how snobbish I can be without knowing it . . .but by the way . . . how are things with you? Is William okay? How is his and your health? What do you hear from my grandchildren?"

"Our health is holding up. William retired last year, and I am about to retire from the corporation. The boys are doing well at college. They come home periodically and seem to be growing into well-rounded individuals like their grandfather!"

"I am still in awe of your meteoric rise to power! I guess they call it CEO in this day and age. That was quite an accomplishment that you did on your own, although I remember coaxing you into majoring in economics along with philosophy. Your hard work paid off handsomely."

"Thanks to you and to Margo."

"Yes, we miss her, don't we? But you have endured your share of grief and life's sorrows compel us to savor the joys that come along. I vividly recall how devastated you were upon learning your friend Dominic was killed in Korea. Recalling that event reminded me of when your mother died. She was the most apolitical person that I ever knew. Remember how she forbade any discussion of the politics or religion, especially at the dinner table?"

"I will forever be indebted to both of you and I will love you both forever!"

"Knowing your origin had no effect on our love for you and your love for us, and that reminds me of why I called - I almost forgot. Do you remember a student of mine named Tobin?.

"Sure, he was in our famous history class!"

"Tobin was in domestic and foreign intelligence services for years. He did some sleuthing for us."

"Did he find anything?"

"He found that your mother died giving birth to you in 1931. She was well liked and respected by her neighbors - your father was unemployed and later gave you up for adoption before enlisting in the Army. He was killed in 1943 during the battle for Guadalcanal and posthumously awarded a Silver Star. I'll send you the written report on all this."

"Thanks, Dad! Those things are important to me."

"Tobin says that he can get that Silver Star sent to you, also."

"That would be wonderful, Dad."

"Well, I better hang up, I'm running out of things to say."

"We must to stay in touch. Are you sure you don't want me to fly out there?"

"No, I'll be fine. Take care of yourselves, I love you!"

Metaphor

SEVERAL ACTORS WITH VARYING degrees of talent rehearsed a play that had been written by the poet Archibald McLeish. The play director attempted to motivate his actors by reading a quote by a noted dramatist, Robert Edmund Jones. It was from a speech given at Yale University. The director paused between each line hoping that the meaning would sink in.

"We are here for a little while between mystery and mystery. We live for a little time on this earth that is so fair - could we sense for a brief moment, the melody of our being - and having sensed it could we impart it to our fellow man?"

Everyone listened politely, some squirming nervously in their seats while others listened pensively. Those thoughts seemed to have little effect until opening night. Then the words of the play were like sharp arrows hurled out at the audience, hitting their mark. The play was based on the Book of Job. There was the wager Satan prompted God to accept, it was a struggle for Job's soul. Some would see it as good versus evil. The audience responded well and sensing that the actors were spurred on to dramatizing more subtle emotions.

A connection was made and maintained between actors and audience. Applause followed the final curtain, and then the audience drifted away, shuffling slowly out of the theater while actors hurried to dressing rooms, removed their make-up and dashed off to a party to celebrate having performed something that some of them did not fully comprehend.

Properties were stowed away for the next performance, except for two large masks used in the play. One of the stage hands mischievously propped them along the backstage wall. There stood the God-mask and the Satan-mask, facing the empty rows of seats in the now silent auditorium. Exit lights above each door muted the darkness aided by one solitary work light above the stage. From silence something is sometimes born. After several minutes a voice came from one of the masks. Then another voice from the other mask responded

"Well!"

"That's a hole in the ground." Then after a short pause,

"That's a line from another play, isn't it?"

"So?"

"Do you have a better one?"

"Yes." There was another pause before the voice assumed a more pretentious tone.

"TO BE OR NOT TO BE, THAT IS THE QUESTION!"

"Hmmm. So?" It grew quiet again for a few minutes.

"What shall we do now?"

"There's not much to do . . . really . . . is there?"

"We can talk to each other."

"We do enough of that during the play, don't we?

"But now we can express our true feelings if we have any!"

"True feelings?"

"If we have any . . . do you have any?".

"Okay, how shall we start?" There was another pause.

"Ahhhhh! I've got it; say one of your lines from the play."

"What for?"

"Oh, just go along with it, don't be such an ass!"

"Like you usually are?"

"Okay. . . .   here   goes . . . "WHENCE COMEST THOU?

"That's my line!

"I know . . . I know . . . you can say mine if you like.

"No, I don't want to be some weird kind of devil!

"Why not, our parts are interchangeable you know. And the Devil is not always weird, is he? Anyway it is a good part and one you also are familiar with, so . . . come on, go on . . . say it!"

"FROM GOING TO AND FRO ON THE EARTH AND FROM WALKING UP AND DOWN IN IT!

"See, that wasn't so bad now, was it?

"What does it mean?"

"What does it mean? It means that you are in it, you are in the earth, you and I are of the earth, you and I like everything and everybody . . .

we . . . everyone comes from the earth . . . or the mind . . . of earth."

"So what? . . . Who really cares about knowing such things?"

"Somebody surely must care . . . sometimes anyway, don't you think? Or do you want to leave all the thinking up to them out there?"

"They are all gone, haven't you noticed?"

"Yes, so what . . . someone must care . . .somewhere!

"I wonder."

"That's part of it. The wonder I mean, don't you see that?"

"Just where are we going with this?"

"We play many roles during our lifetime, just as Shakespeare so eloquently pointed out . . . each of us really is more than one person . . . each of us is truly many people . . . we are protean!"

"Protein?

"No, no, not that kind, you idiot! Proteins are a bunch of amino acids . . . protean . . . means the ability to assume different forms . . . to be changeable, to adapt to circumstances . . . to live!"

"Oh!"

"Yes, to live!"

"Like a skill?"

"Yes, like a skill . . . a habit . . . a talent . . . everyone is really an actor of sorts all the time. . .and usually nobody is ever conscious of their act or their acting!"

"So is that the first mystery?

"Whence comest thou?"

"Yes."

"Hooray! Score one for our side! We've got the answer to that one nailed down, haven't we?"

"Perhaps we do now."

"And what is the last mystery?

"See those exit lights . . . the final mystery is beyond our exit, out there in time and space . . . the endless universe waits!"

"Whose exit?

"Yours. . .mine . . . everybody's."

"That's not in the script! That's some more of that 'Bible-speak' you love to throw around. Go back to the first line!"

"Whence comest thou?"

"Yes."

"It ought to be clear to you now that everyone lives a protean existence assuming various roles, attitudes, manners - habits, oh, yes, tons of habits . . . we become our habits . . . personality grows conditioned by all the impressions registered by slowly maturing brains, conditioned by upbringing, along with the circumstances of time, place, and events."

"So where does that leave us . . . after all, we are just two masks between mysteries. What happens between them?

"Birth and death sandwich existence."

"That is just too much philosophy for me. Cut to the chase!"

"What else do we have?"

"And how else can existence be known and understood?"

"Knowledge is dangerous, isn't it? Remember Eve and her curiosity about that fruit of a certain tree. That got her and Adam discarded from the Garden. But look at it this way, existence normally involves three main elements. There is the body, there is the mind, and there is the soul."

"Soul?"

"Okay, call it spirit."

"You mean the emotions?"

"What is spirit but a much higher level of emotion?"

"Go back a page in your script. For God's sake, just what the devil has the body got to do with it?"

"Remember the director's aim? He told us that we should make the audience feel it in the pit of their stomachs?"

"What? Who?"

"He was talking about how the ideas and emotions of the play should affect the audience, you fool. The actors first have to feel it, and then the audience should feel it the same way, through the body as well as the mind and the emotions."

"Oh, now I get it. You're saying that to really understand anything, one must bring them all together, all three parts.

"Yes . . . in harmony . . .all together."

"And what do you call that, pray tell?"

"That my friend is . . . the melody of being!"

Nora

Soon after the lunch hour ended at the Top Notch, a restaurant much favored by the campus crowd, one of the students working there rushed out. Always in a hurry, he raced across the campus heading toward the library. He was one of the busiest students at the university. In addition to three part time jobs, he studied and drilled with the ROTC, played trombone with a dance band, and occasionally with a small jazz combo. Each of those tasks provided him with funds to pay his tuition as well as room and board. As a senior who would graduate in a few months, he maintained a high grade point average and somehow found time to pitch for the varsity baseball team.

Dominic Callahan sped along paying little attention to where he was going when he fell as he tried to avoid a collision with a coed as he dashed up the library steps. He sprawled on the steps and lay stunned for a moment as he looked up into an attractive face bent over him with a worried frown.

"Are you okay?" he asked the face peering down at him.

"Are you okay?" she asked him while reaching down to help him to his feet.

"I'm sorry . . . I wasn't paying attention." He brushed aside her hand and struggled to his feet.

"Yes, that was quite obvious, but that's not the point. Are you sure you can manage? Shall I call someone for you? You fell pretty darned hard you know?"

"Yes . . . no . . . don't bother, I'll be okay if I can just walk around a minute and get my bearings again!"

"Come on, I'll buy you a cup of coffee while you gather your wits. You aren't one of those clumsy guys from our football team, you know . . . the ones they call 'the stumblers'?"

"No, I'm okay," said Dominic laughing, "I'm not a football player. Baseball is my game . . . and I should buy you the coffee since I almost knocked you down." She laughed.

He limped slightly as they walked to a coffee shop across the street. It was a pleasant experience for him since he seldom had time to date, and she was quite attractive but looked to be somewhat older than most of the coeds on campus.

"I'm working on my masters in Economics," she finally was able to say when he stopped talking for a moment. However Dominic monopolized what passed for conversation, prattling on endlessly about his trombone playing and throwing baseballs while ignoring any mention of academics. Unfortunately, he learned little else about her in his rush to explain himself. She listened patiently as he talked as if he were afraid to stop, nervously conscious of his breathing. They finished their coffee, and she soon disappeared into a crowd of students while he went back to the library to look for the book he needed to read for literature class. It was then that it occurred to him that he had talked so much that he even failed to ask her name.

"What a dumb-ass I am!" he said to no one in particular as he leafed through the book. Then he rushed off again careful not to stumble down the steps of the library. Thirty minutes later he sat in his philosophy class, one of his favorite courses.

Professor Dexter lecture compared Hegel's view of history against Schopenhauer's 'will to live.' Dominic found it difficult to concentrate. The professor's words were like a faint breeze blowing somewhere above him on some different plane. The image of the smiling face that had bent over him and then listened to him spew a torrent of words over a cup of coffee grew steadily in his thoughts.

Several questions occurred to him. Did Schopenhauer really mean 'will to love?' He began to wonder what the young lady was like. He hadn't given her much chance to speak, and he wondered if he should have mustered up the courage to ask for a date. But she was a graduate student, highly intelligent, and probably had plenty of dates already.

After the class ended, he hurried back to tell to his roommate about his encounter on the steps of the library. His roommate, Matt Hughes was a self-proclaimed expert with regard to women. As a talented and ruggedly handsome football player, one of those 'stumblers,' Matt was seldom seen without a girl hanging onto him. He was practically chased by many of the sorority coeds. Dominic told Matt about having coffee with the lady, but Matt had other things on his mind and heard very little of what Dominic was saying.

"Been going with this sweet looking chick for a month now and I still can't get in her pants!" he complained, speaking of his current girl friend. He listed the events they had attended. "I even went to a damned art show with her followed by one of those boring concerts and still no luck! I'm going to give it one more shot and then I'm through with her," he said emphatically.

After supper, Dominic studied for awhile before deciding to relax and sip a few beers at the Top Notch before doing his gig playing with the combo. He hadn't expected to find Matt there, drinking with some other football players. It was crowded as usual, cigarette smoke hung like a dense fog up to the ceiling of the room. Dominic made his way through the throng heading for a seat at the bar when a familiar voice yelled out to him.

"Hey Dom, over here!" It was Matt yelling to him from a booth near the back surrounded by his pals. But sitting next to Matt was a very attractive woman. As he approached the booth, Dominic was startled to see that the young lady was the coed he collided with on the library steps a few hours before. She sat close to Matt, almost snuggling up to him while his arm was draped possessively over her shoulders. Dominic thought that she must be the 'the one and only' who Matt was unable to bed. Now Dominic wished that he could disappear. But it was too late.

"Come here you knuckle-headed, knuckle-ball throwing room-mate! I want you to meet my one and only! Dom, meet Nora . . . Nora this is Dominic, the best pal and roommate in the world! But don't listen to him, he's one of those campus smart guys and he'll just talk your head off!" He motioned one of his comrades to make room for Dominic who now sat nervously beside Nora.

"We've met . . . sort of . . . in a strange way!" chuckled Nora, "We ran into each other on the steps of the library this afternoon. He took a bad tumble so we had a cup of coffee together, and he did talk my head off!" Dominic laughed at the introduction but inside he was furious at Matt, angered by the thought of Matt's hands fondling her. Dominic also grew aware of strong pangs of jealousy.

Regardless, there was now an opportunity to learn more about Nora. She briefly mentioned her plans to travel east to work for a doctorate degree after graduation. As she had turned to Dominic, Matt was lustily gazing at a blond across the aisle. Dominic realized that he liked Nora a great deal, but he soon excused himself and left without finishing his beer. The jazz group he played with was playing at another place down the street, and he hurried off to get his trombone to join them. On his way his thoughts lingered over Nora. As a thousand questions popped into his mind, he could still smell her perfume.

But then playing his trombone would let him escape those thoughts as his attention focused on the music. The group played several numbers, alternating tempos. They had finished an up-tempo medley and began a series of slower, melodic pieces, some of which were from the repertory of the dance band that some of the combo members also played with. These tunes were melancholy and sentimental. Although he preferred the jazzier numbers, he discovered that he now enjoyed playing the romantic tunes a good deal more than before.

They played some Cole Porter tunes, segueing from 'What is This Thing Called Love,' into 'Just One of Those Things,' while Dominic soloed in each. Unsung words of each of the tunes flitted through his brain. It was then that he looked out at the small audience sitting around small tables. Matt and Nora were there, sitting at a table not far from the little stage from which the combo played. When the combo took its break, Dominic felt obligated to go over and sit with Matt and Nora for a few moments carefully masking his feelings and allowing his anger to dissipate.

"I liked that last tune you played very much," said Nora flashing a devastating smile at him, "Does your group play requests? . . .hmm . . . let's see . . . how about Gershwin's 'But Not For Me?' Can you play that for me? Your group is very good you know, and you can probably play that one well, too!"

When the group returned to the stage they opened with Porter's 'Begin the Beguine' followed by Nora's request. Dominic was happy to play for her and grew oblivious of Matt sitting next to her. But he noticed that Matt's arm was not draped over her shoulders as before. The melodies filled the air and several day-dreams about Nora filtered through his thoughts, but they slowly faded as the evening drew to a close.

He almost forgot about her during his busy week ahead, rushing from class to class, drilling with the ROTC, and concentrating on his control during baseball practice. He had planned to give up his part time job at the Top Notch in order to play baseball for this, his final year at the university, but had to continue working to pay for his room and board. Often between innings while pitching at home, his eyes wandered slowly over the spectators along the field hoping to see her. He caught a brief glimpse of her only once, but she had left before the game ended.

Dominic always thought of her whenever he ran up the steps of the library, and even rehearsed what he would say to her if she were to suddenly reappear. But she didn't. His time was spent studying for final exams, and the combo played at the little club only sporadically now. Then one evening there she was. Sitting all alone, listening to him playing. Dominic wondered where Matt was, but he made sure that 'Just One of Those Things' was played. He felt that song whenever he thought of her. After the final set, he joined her at her table.

"Nice to see you!" he said.

"I would have come more often but I had some very serous thinking to do, as well as some serious studying." She looked a bit sad he thought and he waited for her to explain. "I don't know if you know it but Matt stopped calling me. That helped. I was trying to think of some way to tell him anyway."

"Tell him what?"

"That I no longer wanted to be with him."

"Why?"

"There's someone else, someone who probably doesn't know that I exist, or even think about me at all!"

"Really?" Dominic was flustered as it began to dawn on him that she was not only looking right at him, but that she was also talking about him, telling him in her own way how she felt. There was an embarrassing pause. He wanted to say something but the words simply would not come. Then she leaned over and kissed him ever so lightly on the lips. She leaned back, smiling at him. He pulled her close to him. They kissed more deeply this time.

"Let's go somewhere," she whispered in his ear.

"Okay."

She drove them in her car. He sat close to her, trying to breathe her in, almost mesmerized by her presence. He should pinch himself as he mused, "I must be dreaming again!" They parked overlooking the lake just north of town, enjoying the view of the crescent moon's reflection on the dark water. Dominic was pleased with himself because he could enjoy the silence as they watched ripples moving slowly across the water. Talk did not seem to be necessary, and what was there to say? Just being with her was enough for him. But an unspoken understanding grew slowly between them.

They spent several evenings either sitting here by the lake enjoying each other's company or walking along a trail in the woods nearby. He heard music whenever she laughed at something he had said. Then one evening it rained, and instead of coming to the lake, they went to her apartment. She made popcorn and they watched television while making small talk. Their chatter stopped when they embraced. Her smile was different this evening.

Several hours later Nora woke. Dominic was lying asleep next to her in bed. She brushed a tear away from her eyes and quickly dressed. After making breakfast, she woke him. He tiptoed shyly to the bathroom and soon made his way to the table to join her. They exchanged smiles and ate without saying a word, pausing occasionally to briefly hold hands. Time seemed to hang quietly waiting for them to enjoy.

The days slipped by all too quickly. Their stay at the university was coming to an end. One sunny morning over four hundred students received their diplomas. He watched as she received her master's degree before he moved slowly across the same platform in the huge gymnasium to receive his bachelor's degree. He wore his Army uniform, the gold bars of a second lieutenant on his shoulders twinkled under the stage lights. A frown accompanied him across the stage that lasted until his eyes met hers as he was on his way back to his seat. She was smiling at him and he happily returned it with a wink.

Their last night together had been wonderful and sad at the same time. After graduation ceremonies, she came to say goodbye before driving east to work on her doctorate at Harvard. Dominic was going to board a train heading west to Fort Riley, Kansas, for tactical field training. They embraced warmly and each pulled back to look at the other. They knew that they would not be seeing each other for a long time. Finally it was she who spoke first

"Write!"

"No tears!" Dominic smiled at her as his arms held her gently and he again felt the warmth of her lips.

"I love you!" she said, smiling up at him.

His smile faded and he looked at her again, almost afraid to take his eyes away from her. He wanted desperately to remember her as she was then, and stared at her as if his eyes were a camera lens recording a picture forever.

"I love you too, Nora! I love you very much!"

She smiled at him once more. An unexplainably strange feeling of dread came over her for a moment. It was a strange disquieting premonition which she quickly shunted aside. She took a deep breath before regaining her composure and smiled again.

"Come back safely," she whispered, "there is so much to do and I will be waiting for you."

"I know, I will!" said Dominic. He turned and walked slowly away wanting to turn back, wanting to stay with her, but now he couldn't. Duty called. But he did turn to look back for one more glance at her. For just a moment. She too had stopped and turned again to look back at him. That was the last time they would ever see each other.

She was smiling and waving to him.

He smiled and waved at her.

Over the Line

THE COLD POINT OF a steel bayonet was just an inch away from Orin Fitzgerald's neck, close to his jugular vein. Flat on his back he stared wide-eyed up into the muzzle of his rifle to which the bayonet was affixed. It was now menacing his prone body while a combat boot nudged his crotch. At the other end of Orin's Garand rifle the scowling face of Sergeant Harlan Griswold glared down at him. Griswold was one of the bayonet instructors at Fort McClellan, Alabama.

It was autumn, 1946. The shooting war ended the year before but here at the Infantry Replacement Training Center the usual methods of preparing men for combat were still the order of the day. Only a few moments before, Orin had brandished his bayoneted rifle, poking it with only slight enthusiasm toward Griswold who was urging Orin to stick him with it.

"Come on, Fitzgerald; try to stick me with that goddamned thing! What are you one of them sissy mama's boys! Fight like your life is on the line . . . you slimy bastard!" But Orin was hesitant until Griswold prodded him further using other words, "Think of me as some buck nigger raping your lily pure wife!" An infuriated Orin lunged at the red-neck instructor. But Griswold had used the same ploy with other recruits and was prepared for their reaction while welcoming their anger. He had worked with the "steel" as he called it many times and used it effectively since returning from Guadalcanal where he killed several Japanese soldiers with it, garnering multiple Bronze Stars plus a Purple Heart. He was the consummate soldier – thoroughly trained, toughened to endure hardship, and able to prevail and kill. He was good at that.

The angry Fitzgerald moved quickly toward Griswold and made a wild but vicious thrust clearly meant to do bodily harm. But Griswold side-stepped Orin's bayonet deftly, which sliced into empty air. With lightning speed Griswold stepped close to Orin, grabbed Orin's rifle and twisted it from him while roughly shoving him down onto the red Alabama soil, ending with the point of the blade sticking into it instead of Orin's neck.

"That's how you gotta do it in close combat or your ass is dead!" Griswold paused to catch his breath, "Shit, most of the time you can't see the whites of their goddamned eyes! But sometimes . . . sometimes . . . you find them bastards right in your face and steel is the only answer to that kind of shit!" He paused and in his condescending way, he stared at the platoon of recruits now watching him with fascination. He was an arrogant man, sorry that the war had ended. He relished fighting the way small children relish Christmas, missing the pungent odor of cordite and putrid blood that leavened the soil after combat. Griswold missed the powerful feeling of living close to death that co-existed with his hidden unconscious fears.

"Any questions?" he growled at the rookies. Rodney Pearson's hand shot up in the second row. He was a nice young man from Jackson, Mississippi. He came from a wealthy family, his father being a lawyer and all.

"Does the bayonet ever get stuck? . . . I mean, mine got stuck in one of the dummies we practiced on this morning . . . so what do you do then, huh, sergeant?"

"Ask your drill instructor, Sergeant Landon over there. He landed with the first wave at Anzio, and got his ass shot up, but not before he stuck a couple of them goddamned Krauts with his steel! He'll tell you how!" Landon, who had been standing in back of his platoon watching the demonstration, came forward.

He stood quietly for a moment collecting what had to be unpleasant thoughts. He was not like Griswold; he despised the war and everything connected with it. He tried civilian life for a short time but reluctantly re-enlisted and became a drill instructor because he didn't see much else to do with his life. Besides, as an alcoholic he needed the discipline that he could only find in the Army. Now he frowned as a scene played again in his mind.

"The battalion hadn't moved very far that day when my squad was sent ahead to recon Germans, find out where they were dug in. They weren't too far away. I ran along and jumped into this trench only to find a Kraut with his pants down taking a shit, and before I could even think, my bayonet was sticking in his chest. Before he died, that damned Kraut farted and stunk up the whole god dammed trench." Gales of laughter erupted from the men in the platoon who sat on the ground listening.

"Shut the fuck up!" yelled Griswold. Landon paused until the laughter faded away. He also was not amused at their reaction and stared at them sternly before continuing, "But the god damned bayonet was stuck in him so good that it was a bitch to get out. I was standing there in that smell until I remembered what my bayonet instructor back at Fort Bragg told me months before. So, I pulled the trigger and the rifle's recoil shoved the damned rifle and the bayonet out of the dead Kraut and back into my hands . . . easy as pie!"

The rookie they called Blackie because of his deep dark tan was almost as dark as a Negro was stunned. He was a sensitive young man from Ohio. Sitting in the first row he watched the gleam in Griswold's eyes, and realized that if Orin was a Negro that he'd be a dead man by now. Griswold's manner and his words bore testimony of his hatred of Negroes that became evident to Blackie. After their five-minute break, the soldiers returned to the bayonet course and 'attacked' all the dummies. Some were propped up in trenches; some hung from large 'A' frames, and a few had been placed along low wooden walls. The members of the platoon now responded with greater vigor than they displayed during their morning session.

While most of the rookies in this training platoon were teenagers, Orin was a good deal older. Son of a sharecropper in Georgia, his had been a life of misery and pain. His father, Carnell, beat both him and his mother mercilessly whenever he drank too much, something he often did. Then he 'turned nasty.' Once Orin stood between his drunken father and his weeping mother, fending off blows until one knocked him clear across the room of the shack in which they and his siblings lived.

Orin was the oldest of seven children, but three had died during infancy. Food had been scarce whenever the crops failed, and many times they had eaten grass and stringy roots dug from the ground near their shack. When his father was killed in an accident, Orin became the head of the family and was deferred in the draft that took many young men off to die in foreign lands during the great war. Yet Orin wanted desperately to get away from the life of a sharecropper. He decided to become a soldier, having seen some near Fort

Benning not far from his home and having been impressed by their uniform and swagger.

Since lying is sometimes the only action possible for the desperate, Orin altered his birth certificate to show that he was ten years younger than he was. He was really thirty-nine years old. After joining the platoon, he was surprised to find just how much the difference age mattered as he worked diligently to keep up with the youthful members of the platoon. Most of them scampered through the obstacle courses like fun-loving monkeys, relishing their energy and what it allowed them to do. Orin was always last in such exercises, and became a burden to his squad while doing the 'log drill.' Yet he stubbornly plodded on sweating profusely, refusing to give up. He had other secrets as well.

Once when he was a small boy he wandered into the town a few miles away from where he lived. He found the small library in town to his liking. It became a haven of sorts. He began reading every book he could. By doing that relentlessly over those childhood years, Orin grew intellectually far beyond the few years of school he was allowed to attend. All hands in the family were needed in the field and going to school was out of the question most of the time for sharecropper children. But his informal learning paid an unexpected dividend of sorts when he enlisted in the Army. Orin scored extremely high on the Army General Classification Test.

None of that meant much to Sergeant Landon or any of the other basic training instructors at Fort McClellan. The only intelligence they were concerned with was how well each recruit obeyed instructions; how well they could do close order drills, field exercises, and their scores on the rifle range. Except for the obstacle courses, Orin was rapidly becoming a favorite of not only the instructors but also of the members of his platoon. They slowly grew to respect this quiet man who they often referred to as 'Pops,' but not in his presence after he glared at one of them after doing so. So they called him 'Fitz.'

He performed very well on the rifle range with skills he learned squirrel hunting back home. His rapid fire with the Garand rifle at two-hundred yards gleaned him a perfect score, and no one in the entire training battalion of a thousand men had done that. His other scores in every firing position were also high and he earned the rating of expert rifleman. In time he also mastered the bayonet. Instructors never challenged him again after he disarmed one who challenged him as Sergeant Griswold had. Orin allowed himself to be thrown as before, but this time he rolled quickly over as the bayonet thrust by his instructor struck the Alabama soil. Orin leaped to his feet, wrestled the instructor to the ground with an arm-lock, threw him to the ground and stood over him triumphantly with a foot on the prone body.

During off-duty hours, recruits were not permitted to leave the company area except during the final week of training. Day 'passes' were allowed to recruits but only after each soldier desiring one reported to the company orderly room looking spick and span in Class-A Khaki uniform. One Sunday afternoon Orin trailed along with Rodney and Blackie as they visited the nearby town of Aniston. It was there at a USO club that Orin appreciated Blackie more while growing aware of Rodney's prejudice. They sat at a table drinking Coca-Colas with a pretty young hostess who enjoyed interrogating her soldier guests, often asking each what state they haled from.

"Where y'all from, soldier?" she asked Blackie who was sitting to her left feeling important because she spoke to him first.

"Ohio."

"Oh, so you're a Yankee, then!"

"Yup, guess so," he smiled.

"A damned Yankee, huh?"

"I guess so," he replied sheepishly as if that were bad.

"Are you one of them nigger lovers?"

Blackie was perplexed. What was she trying to make him say? Frustrated, he struggled to come up with an answer. Mixed feelings overcame him for a moment. On the one hand he had no special love of Negroes having been around only a few during his seventeen years. Yet he remembered seeing those miserable shacks along the tracks as his train rolled through the south on the way to Fort McClellan. He was told that the shacks were where the 'nigras lived'. Somewhere deep within him empathy for the downtrodden had been a part of him and he looked at those shacks with a good deal of sorrow. His smile was gone when he turned back to look into the eyes of the girl.

"Yeah!" he finally said, "I love 'em, so what's it to you?"

"I declare!" she said, surprised, "I never before met anyone so rude as to even admit to such a thing! You need to mind your manners, ya hear?" She rose and strode away angrily. It was then that Rodney's anger surfaced.

"What did you say such a stupid thing for?"

"It wasn't stupid . . . she was for showing off!"

"You damned Yankees need to be taught a lesson . . . you went over the line . . . and I suppose that I'm just the guy who can do it!"

Orin interceded. Rodney seemed to calm down but only for a minute. Then his face flushed red with anger. He wanted to fight Blackie, show him a thing or two as he put it.

"Listen, you two," said Orin, "Stay out of trouble! If them there Military Policemen standing outside catch you guys dukin' it out here in town you'll both wind up having to do the whole damned basic training all over again like Sergeant Landon said when he told us we could have passes this weekend, remember?"

Rodney persisted and by the time the trio returned to the camp, Blackie agreed to fight Rodney. The fisticuffs would take place in the space between two of the tar papered barracks. They changed into fatigue uniforms, stripped to the waist, and were about to begin throwing punches when Sergeant Landon appeared. He sent another soldier to fetch boxing gloves while a small crowd from their squad and another from their platoon formed the 'ring' in which the fight would take place. Some agreed with Rodney after being told of the incident at Aniston, while others didn't care one way or another. No one sided with Blackie except Orin who stood in Blackie's corner giving encouraging advice. Landon told one of the other soldiers with a wrist watch to time each round.

There was yet another secret that Orin had been keeping to himself. Besides the date of birth, he had also altered the word 'Caucasian' on his birth certificate. He was three generations removed from a white man whose name was Fitzgerald, an Irish reprobate who married, or lived with, Orin's great-grandmother for several years. Some of that genetic background was kind to him, and his facial features were neutral although he was deeply tanned.

But there was a good deal of Negro blood flowing through his veins despite the fact that his features allowed him to pass for a white man. That permitted him to use the library in that small town near his home in Georgia when he was a boy. He knew his appearance would allow him to join the Army, and he did not regret lying about his race, or his age, or his lack of formal schooling.

The fight went on for several rounds. Rodney and Blackie slammed their fists against each other's body several times each round leaving noticeable welts. Self-righteousness fueled his anger, which had not diminished in the least. Blackie was simply angered by Rodney's taunts. Sweating profusely, their faces became red with each stinging blow of the gloves. Rodney took pleasure in hitting, but enjoyed enjoy being struck as well for deep within him lurked a strange sense of guilt. Eventually they were exhausted, but neither would give up. Both were relieved when Landon stopped the fight. He made them shake hands, took their gloves, and walked away smiling and smoking a cigarette.

A few days later the recruits assembled at the amphitheater by the railroad tracks, sitting in the hot sun waiting for instructions to board trains taking them home for a brief visit before heading to their new assignments. The new soldiers of the entire battalion of four companies were assigned to different camps around the country. Some would 'ship out,' joining overseas units of occupying forces in Germany or Japan. Rodney went home to Mississippi before heading to California, slated for overseas duty, but there he got into a fight and accidentally killed a sailor in San Francisco. He went to prison at Fort Leavenworth instead. Blackie headed for Ohio and then to Camp Stoneman, shipped over to Korea and served out his enlistment.

Orin wasn't far from his home in Georgia, and from there went to OCS, Officers Candidate School, and became a second lieutenant. A few years later in 1950, he was sent to Korea following the invasion of South Korea by the communists. But now there was shooting war going on, the one that Sergeant Landon promised: "there's always gonna be a war someplace, sometime, so be ready! Learn all you can about soldiering, you may need it sooner than you think!"

The North Korean Army had swept south over-running and conquering almost all of the entire peninsula, forcing defenders into what was called the Pusan Perimeter, a small corner in the southeastern part of the nation near the port city bearing the same name. American Army units stationed from Japan had been rushed to the aid of the South Koreans and were the mainstay of the defensive line when Orin arrived in July.

The assault on Pusan was relentless and grew to a ferocious intensity. When Orin took his platoon on patrol he gave his men the order "fix bayonets," but they were used mostly to open cans of "C Rations." Marching through the countryside he observed that Korean peasants lived in conditions similar to sharecroppers he knew back in Georgia. Later when his unit was in the thick of several battles they suffered many casualties. Bayonets proved to be cumbersome and were generally left in sheathes fastened to the web belts wore by all infantry soldiers.

Orin's bravery under fire was never acknowledged for soon after he pulled several wounded men from out of the line of fire, machine gun bullets ripped through him. His platoon had engaged a company of North Koreans near a place called Taegu in October. His death occurred almost four years to the day after he completed basic training at Fort McClellan.

Peanut butter and jelly . . .

BILLY CRANDALL AND JIMMY Pearson were cousins. They looked and often acted alike. People remarked that they were 'peas from the same pod.' Both boys enjoyed a close relationship because of their abiding friendship. Billy's mother Helen, and Jimmy's mother Mildred were sisters whose family tree stretched far back into history to what had been a more 'delicious time' before anti-bellum days ended. But Helen and Mildred only heard stories about those times from their grandparents. Helen married a local doctor in the small town thirty miles away from Jackson where Mildred settled with her husband, a prominent attorney.

The boy cousins spent a good deal of time together while growing up although one lived in the city and the other in a small town. But Jimmy spent most summer months and many weekends at Billy's home and the Crandall family because Mildred thought that small town living was better for his upbringing. Helen agreed heartily and the two boys normally played from morning until night each summer day stopping only to enjoy their favorite snack, peanut butter and jelly sandwiches washed down with large glasses brim full of cool lemonade.

Helen Crandall enjoyed preparing the snacks for the boys, but she was not always aware when the boys taunted each other by making faces while sitting at the breakfast table eating their meals, often opening their mouths displaying huge gobs of a gooey mess. This caused a great deal of squealing laughter which exasperated Mrs. Crandall, but boys will be boys, she thought.

"Gotcha last!" one would yell at the other.

"Uh-uh!" was the equally loud response.

"Eat your sandwiches, boys and stop acting the fool!" interjected Mrs. Crandall whenever she became aware of their activity behind her back. But her oft repeated exhortations didn't stop them. The boys continued with such deliberate teasing even after reaching their teens. It had become a joyful ritual for them, one that they could not easily abandon. Still, despite their uncanny resemblance, each boy developed his own character and his own personality.

Billy was somewhat introverted, cautious and quiet especially when his partner in fun was not around. Jimmy was more out-going and the obvious leader in these forays into their playful 'madness.' Eventually Billy preferred to be called Bill and Jimmy preferred being Jim, but to their parents and others in the neighborhood they remained Billy and Jimmy to everyone despite their occasional protests.

They were constant companions, riding their bicycles all over the small town. Sometimes they merely wandered about with no apparent destination in mind. When they were younger they followed the railroad tracks several miles out of town in each direction seeking adventure. Occasionally they hiked out past shanty-town, shed their clothing and went skinny dipping in the cool water of the river. There were usually older boys there. Some of them already had public hair or signs of it appearing on their smooth bodies. Billy and Jimmy could hardly wait until they too possessed this growth signifying approaching manhood, and they happily joined the rowdier boys who gathered in a circle by the river bank stoking their members to see which could make it spit further than the others.

When their wanderlust of exploring the town subsided, they simply played in the Crandall's expansive back yard while waiting for their favorite snack to appear. The yard contained several large trees but the largest was their usual target. They climbed up as far into the many branches as they could, or swung gleefully on a tire hung from the strongest limb, all the while screaming with joy and stopping only when Mrs. Crandall appeared with those delicious peanut butter and jelly sandwiches. The years rolled by almost unnoticed except something gradually took place although it was quite imperceptible and less understood. Their closeness seemed to change slightly as though something was pulling them apart while they continued their usual manner of play. But time has its ways of altering everyone in varying degrees, some less subtle than others. It became obvious during one of Jimmy's frequent weekend visits to the Crandall home during the school year. One Sunday morning after Jimmy had washed and dressed he called to Billy who still languished in bed.

"Come on wise-guy, time to get up and go to church."

"Ain't going," came Bill's muffled voice from under the covers before poking his head out to say, "You go on ahead," then after a pause, "I'll see you later maybe."

"What's the matter, you aren't turning into one of them heathens or some such thing, are you?" said Jim laughing.

"Naw."

"What then? Your folks will be fit to be tied."

"They know."

"They know what?"

"It's that Sunday school teacher we got," said the muffled voice again under the covers, "All he talks about is sin . . . and 'bominations . . . stuff like that . . . all that stuff just makes me feel creepy. . . makes my blood boil . . . that's all there is to it."

"Shucks, Bill, 'taint but an hour or so. Can't you stand to hear about a little sin for such a little bitty time? Come on, get up, will you? I want you to go with me." But Bill didn't move and Jim kept pleading with him to no avail.

"Aw, come on Bill, get your butt out of bed and come with me!" Jim was annoyed and waited a few more minutes before quietly leaving the room. He went to Sunday school without Bill for the first time ever.

Yet their personalities were somehow complimentary, each bringing out the opposite in the other. Somehow they fit together. They were really two peas in a pod. They each were more like a whole person until Jim went back to Jackson. But after that time that Bill refused to go to church with him, things between them gradually changed. The changes seemed to emanate from Bill, and there was something he was reluctant to talk about.

Jim somehow sensed that during a visit later that year. Both had just graduated from high school. They sat in the Crandall summer kitchen eating peanut butter and jelly sandwiches. They had recently stopped their habit of making faces at each other while eating. Today Jim made a half-hearted attempt doing that but Bill turned away from him scowling.

"What are doing that crazy stuff for, huh?"

"What's wrong, Bill, you ain't your normal self no more?"

"What do you mean by normal?" he said angrily rising from the table as if to leave. His face was flushed and he was upset about something. But he slowly took his seat and mumbled what was meant to be an apology. He always had strong feelings for Jim and realized that he shouldn't be flying off the handle when Jim was simply being Jim.

"Didn't mean nothing, don't get on your high horse or else I'll have to put you down," Jim said laughing. The room grew quiet, and Jim was still concerned about Bill but tried to keep it hidden. He would try another tack.

"You aren't sick, are you?" after a short pause.

"Nope."

"Then what is it? You seem like you're down in the dumps all the darned time when I come over here. You been this way the last few times." He paused, studying Bill's face looking for some kind of an answer, "I know you Bill, and I know that something's pretty damned wrong. Something's gotta be wrong . . . right?" Jim looked out the window and took a deep breathe.

"Is there anything I can do? Can I do something to make you feel like the old Bill that I know?"

"You can just stop yakking at me, that's what you can do!"

"I'm not yakking at you, I just want to help!"

"Just, shut up!" yelled Bill, his facer reddening, "Just shut the hell up!" It was clear that the persistent questioning by Jim only made Bill angrier. So Jim stopped questioning him altogether but he remained bewildered by Bill's manner. Finally after several minutes of eerie silence, Bill spoke softly and hesitantly of his visit to Atlanta a few weeks before.

"Father went to a medical convention there, and he made me go along . . . I didn't want to . . . but he made me and while we were there somethin' happened . . ." his voice trailed off. Bill obviously had some bad experience and had difficulty in relating it to Jim. Part of him wanted to confess, but another part didn't. Then finally after a long quiet moment, Bill spoke again.

"I had to see a head doctor."

"A psycho guy?"

"Yeah."

"So what? No big deal. Lots of folks talk to them." Jim now began to look worried, "You aren't no psycho!" He felt empathetic and wanted to find some way to make Bill feel better, but all he could do was listen as Bill explained.

"He told me that I have . . . these tendencies."

"What tendencies?" Bill swallowed and looked Jim squarely in the face as his eyes filled with tears. He sat still and was very quiet before speaking again; almost weeping as he did. He almost spit out the word that sounded harsh and cruel.

"Homo . . . homosexual!"

If a pin dropped at that moment one would have heard it clearly. The silence that followed stunned them both as the meaning of his words sank in. Jim dropped his peanut butter and jelly sandwich. A look of horror crossed his face, which quickly turned red with rage.

"What the hell are you saying? Are you turning into one of them goddamned queers? . . . Are you? . . . Jesus Christ? . . . tell me!" Bill rose and started to leave the room but Jim grabbed him and shoved him roughly back into his chair.

"Tell me . . . that you are not . . . one . . . of them goddamned queers! . . . How long has this been going on for Christ's sake? Tell me!" Bill sat saying nothing but nodded quietly.

Bill rose and stood near Jim, his hand on Jim's shoulder.

"Don't touch me! Get your damned hand off me!" The pitch of Jim's voice was rising and he was almost screaming.

Bill took his hand away and looked at it.

"Why are you doing this to me?" yelled Jim jumping up from his chair, his voice returning to his normal baritone, "Why are you doing this to all of us? Goddamnit, Bill! Why are you doing this to . . . your family. . . to our family? Why, dammit! . . . Why?" Bill slowly looked up. His face was twisted by a pain that Jim could not understand.

"I can't help it I guess. There is nothing that we. . . I can do about it. That's what the doctor said." He stood and moved toward Jim who recoiled a few steps back as if Bill had some contagious disease.

"This screws up everything! Jim yelled, "You know that don't you? This screws up everything! We are done for! You and I are done for!" He went to the door, and turned to look back at Bill one last time, "I never want to see your queer ass again! You gotta go away, you just gotta go away!" Jim raced out of the room crying. Bill's confession had affected him. Not only would he not visit again, he began using his middle name, Rodney instead of his first name, James. He joined the Army and left for training in Alabama without saying goodbye to anyone.

Tension in the Crandall house grew. His mother didn't know of Bill's condition at first or even his talk with the psychiatrist, until several days had elapsed. Then she saw only the strange torment in Bill's expression. Meanwhile his father would sit grim-faced at supper, refusing to answer Helen's sobbing questions. Then finally he shared the secret with her. Eventually Bill took his meals in the summer kitchen away from them.

The days moved along slowly. Bill grew more isolated. When walking down the street he was certain that everybody in the whole town knew his secret, that he was queer. Everybody must despise me, he thought. He felt as though he was in some kind of a prison. And it hurt whenever he thought of his friend Jim and their last meeting. But actually very few people in town knew his secret.

One afternoon Bill even went to see the preacher at the church he had grown to despise.

"What can I do, Reverend Dodd? What can I do? Can you help me, my parents won't even talk with me anymore, and my best friend Jim is gone away to the Army! I am all alone in this world . . . am I to live that way forever?"

"Son, please tell me what on earth is bothering you?"

"It's one of them 'bominations you spoke of, I have become one of those 'bominations!"

"How do you know, Billy? . . . How do you know that?"

"Went to Jackson with my father and he had me talk with a doctor who is a psychiatrist . . . he told me."

"Do you believe in him more than in our Lord Jesus?"

"I don't know what to believe! What am I to do?"

"Pray, son! Pray with all your might! And the Lord will heal you. You need come to church every Sunday . . . you need to pray more! You must turn away from such temptations . . . turn to God, he will heal you through divine providence.

Of that there can be no doubt! Then you will be made whole again!"

Billy walked home slowly. He would try to pray, but when he did strange thoughts popped into his head. Visions of hell and damnation fueled his imagination. He wanted to cry out but no sound came from him as he lay in bed that night. He got up and kneeled by his bed but there was no comfort in praying. Instead he remembered all the fun he and Jimmy had, exploring the town, following the railroad tracks, skinny dipping in the river. He shuddered as he recalled becoming aroused while watching Jimmy come out of the water. His muscular tanned body was taunt, the skin smooth like silk.

Meanwhile the guilt and anger that seemed to have frozen his father's tongue subsided. He and Billy's mother had a long talk and began to understand that they needed to accept their son rather than shun him. Helen Crandall planned to do that the very next day after she made him a peanut butter and jelly sandwich. At that moment Billy was at the end of the back yard, sitting in the swing made from an old automobile tire hanging from the largest tree in the yard. Jimmy and he had swung on it many times, laughing and joyfully yelling at each other.

Tears filled Billy's eyes. He took his pocket knife and slowly cut the sturdy rope letting the tire drop off. Using his knowledge of rope tying he learned as a Boy Scout, he fashioned a loop at the end of the rope. Then he stopped and looked around at the yard and the big house searching for memories that would not appear. He climbed up into their favorite tree just as he had done many time with Jimmy in the wonderful days now gone forever. Slowly and methodically Billy pulled the noose over his head while standing on a sturdy branch several feet above the ground.

He yanked the rope tight before stepping off the branch. Hardly any sound came from him. It was about then that Helen Crandall came from the house with a peanut butter and jelly sandwich on a small plate. Tears filled her eyes as she wondered just what she would say to Billy and was hoping that the peanut butter and jelly would display the love she still felt for her son despite his "transgression." She had almost passed the tree when she looked up. Helen Crandall stopped dead in her tracks. A horrible scream left her throat. Looking up she saw Billy's lifeless body dangling from his favorite tree.

Que sera sera
By Augustus Leary

THIS IS MY 'TERM paper,' see? Let me tell you how this all came about. Here goes . . . crazy questions and crazy answers, that's what I got when I went to night school. See, my old lady is a school teacher and I never got to finish high school. One day she said I should go to these classes given for adults like me. Besides, if it made her happy why shouldn't I? She said I could learn something maybe. How can you argue with that?

Now I'm not some dumb-bell but I am past forty so I figured that I qualify as an adult now and maybe she's right. It sure couldn't hurt. So, I went and to my surprise, I learned lots more than I ever thought I could. You should never stop learning. That's a big order, huh? Up to now all I learned besides the box scores in the paper is whose running at the track. But in school it was a whole lot different.

There were all these questions I never thought of. Who wrote the Declaration of Independence? And why? What caused the World War? Who did what to whom? And why are we here? And who are we? What is the meaning of life? What the hell is protoplasm? Who was the fourteenth president? Those things and other even more aggravating stuff came up in those classes. I don't know why, but they did. And you know what? I sort of liked thinking about that stuff. I had never done much of that all my life. Got me to thinking that maybe everybody but me thought about such things. Maybe. Maybe not. Anyways, if the lectures got too boring one could always take a short snooze if you take a seat in the back row. That's what I did.

First let me tell you some things about myself. My name is Augustus, but don't ever call me that. Call me Gus. I drive a hack in the city. Doing that for a long time. You also get an education driving a cab all over town with all kinds of people sitting back there behind you in the back seat. Some never say a peep. Others jabber away all the time saying things no sane person should have to think about or hear.

Hell, I'm pretty sure that God was a passenger in my cab once. Big guy. Yeah. Got in back there and sat like a king or something. And I could just feel him sitting back there even when I didn't look in the mirror. Especially when I didn't look in the mirror. I just knew he was there. Says to me to take him to the 'place' and you know what? I knew exactly what he meant without even asking. So I turned the heap around and headed for the place where the Towers used to be, knowing somehow that he wanted to see it.

I was just pulling up to the curb and looked out my window to see him already walking away, walking right toward it. I hadn't even heard the door open and I was just about to yell at him for skipping on the fare when my right hand found a twenty laying on the seat next to me. God was a good tipper that's for sure. But I had other strange rides. Once a guy sitting in the back sticks a gun through the opening and yells he wants all my money. Fuck him I thought and shoved the thirty-eight I always carry for such emergencies right back into his face. He left in a hurry with no cash. He left the damned door open on his way though. God, that pissed me off!

Now my mother taught me not to take any crap from people so that's where I get all that foolish bravery. She was a tough old bird and my father was no slouch either. He was a longshoreman who occasionally hit the bottle. Well, actually he lived off the sauce most of the time. What the hell, those guys working the docks go through hell to make a living! I suppose you have to cut them some slack, right?

When he got soused he always found a way to sneak in and drop himself in the sack. He had to learn how to sneak in because once he came home snookered and Mama heard him stumbling near the kitchen door. She cold-cocked him right there saying I'm not going to bed with a stinking drunk, you can sleep it off here in the kitchen. He did.

My father woke up the next morning still on the kitchen floor but my mother had covered him with a couple of blankets and even stuck a pillow under his head. That's love, man. And they never fought over religion considering their backgrounds. He was Catholic. She was Jewish, and so I got to check out both religions being dragged off to Temple one day and off to Mass another. All in the same week mind you! So I can vouch for the fact that mixed marriages do work. I grew to like those Catholic Micks. The Jewish kids were okay, too. But that's life growing up in the city. Anyway my parents they gave me a good upbringing which my old lady now augments by telling me all kinds of stuff and sending me off to adult school.

So where was I? Oh, yeah. Questions and answers. Like there are lots more questions that you can imagine. The answers can drive you up the wall as well. Turns out that we are something called homo-sapiens, closely related to, or similar to, depending on your religion, monkeys. They are called primates. People are supposed to be primates but my experience driving the hack tells me that most of them don't act like primates, they really act more like second-ates, and maybe even third-ates or fourth-ates! I think that I've seen them all.

Anyhow, we may have come from out there someplace in space. That's what a guy named Carl Sagan said in a book he wrote, which we had to read from out loud for crying out loud. In it he says that we were all made of 'star stuff.' Now what the hell do you make of that? What does all of that mean? Another guy said that we can never know the universe and the Rabbi said that God cannot be known by us since we are merely humans. So maybe they are the same thing, no?

Sometimes when laying in bed before going to sleep I try to imagine the whole damned thing, our solar system, the Milky Way and thousands of galaxies strewn all over the heavenly sky. I have not been successful in this attempt, but I'll tell you this, it sure can give you one helluva headache if you keep at it for more than an hour like I did that one night. I will not do that again. Hell, I gotta get up early and read the Times before I get behind the wheel. There's a lot to learn from reading a newspaper but you need to get past the crap, and believe me there is crap all over the place, not only in newspapers but out there on the streets. I suppose it seeps up over the countryside as well but since I haven't driven further than Jersey in my cab I can't say.

Speaking of Jersey, for example, one day this lummox jumps into my cab and wants to go to Jersey. Princeton I think. When I tell him the fare he about craps all over the back seat jumping up and down bitching at me so I not too politely ask him to get the hell out of my cab, which he does and then kicks the side door. That hurt his foot more than the cab, which I really do not own anyways so to hell with him.

Getting back to school. I am slowly learning a bunch of stuff. The mind is like a full bladder filled with lots of crazy thoughts that don't mean doodley damn. If you aren't careful some of that crap leaks out of your head and slips into your mouth if you are not careful. Then you will let everybody know what a jerk you can be a times. It is amazing just how the mind can screw up your life if you don't pay attention. That's the lesson. Pay attention!

Wish I'd had gone to this school before the Army grabbed my ass and hauled it off to Vietnam. That happened just after I graduated from reform school. Hell I didn't know what side was up let alone ever have heard of Vietnam. Luckily, the shooting was winding down when I got there and the worst I got was a bit of shrapnel in the leg. Had I been really paying attention I would been ducking for cover like the smart guys did.

So what I learned was this - most of the time people are somnambulistic. That's a pretty big word for a guy like me, but the instructors at school liked to use big words. Come to think of it in the Army anybody using them was either a West Pointer or an asshole bull-shitter! Another thing, look at how inside the atom electrons orbit around that thing in the middle. If you could see it, you'd see the solar system is like that, stuff flying around other stuff. I've seen pictures of what scientists think the universe looks like, been going on longer than the Bible says!

I think religions missed the damned boat, they got some emotional diarrhea or some such thing. Some are mad at gays and lesbians. They never started a war! How about them Buddhists, they never started a war, huh? Did they? Why do some people think they have all the answers to everything, and want to tell others how to live? What I'm looking for is the real McCoy so's I can be part of what's going on and not be just another victim.

Reunion

THE LETTER FROM THE university lay unopened on Tobin's desk for several days. Reluctantly he opened it. It's probably another request for money, that's usually what they wanted. Instead he discovered an announcement about the reunion of his graduating class. He frowned while reading, but not because of the letter. He had just returned from the dentist and the numbing effect of Novocain was wearing off. His jaw throbbed painfully.

He sat for a moment trying to recall faces of those that were in his class. There were several he liked, and more that he didn't much care for. It takes all kinds to make a world he thought as he put the letter down. He had met lots of people during his years at the university and now he recalled that he had known little about them beyond the awareness that they were creatures who occasionally occupied space near him. That was enough, he thought at the time.

During his college days Tobin observed that the goal of many students was to graduate and leverage their education into making a fortune. He envisioned them now as having found a comfortable niche in corporate America, wallowing in wealth and now living happily ever after, golfing away retirement years somewhere in Florida or Arizona. Education for them was a means to an end, but Tobin always felt that it was an end in itself. He had struggled to understand himself and find some meaning in his life. Quite often he sat in his college dormitory room pausing during his studies to wonder if there any purpose in life beyond securing creature comforts. He saw that he was still struggling even now to separate reality from illusion.

Elective courses appealed to Tobin during his college days and he chose history and philosophy. These along with his required classes in psychology proved to be interesting and useful all his life. He often took courses others had cautioned him to avoid, courses taught by professors who were considered by campus wizards as 'tough graders. Professor Dexter was one of those he was told to avoid at all costs. But Tobin chose Dexter's classes anyway and found them both informative and perplexing. The professor often scrawled quotations on the blackboard in the classroom.

"Write this little gem down on a slip of paper somewhere, stick it in your pocket and from time to time take it out and read it. See if it makes sense to you. Try to understand it but don't be surprised if it takes some time to really understand it fully," he warned. "If you still can't figure out what it means, you can always bring it up during a 'free for all' session," referring to the time each week when students were encouraged to express views on any subject in sort of a helter-skelter manner that students always enjoyed.

Tobin thrived on the mental challenges but found them as puzzling as those quotations on slips of paper in his jacket pocket. With the professor's prompting he began to see connections everywhere, especially those that slid into gray areas of abstraction that usually flew over his head during lectures. Some were easy to ignore or forget. Tobin saw that history was more than stories about the past. It revealed a remarkable progression with innovations in thinking which propelled every civilization in varying degrees. He breezed through higher mathematics of his engineering courses but found greater challenge with difficult questions posed by philosophy.

He fought against self doubts and low self esteem and went beyond accumulating information and sought to understand himself and the world around him. And while he felt somewhat alienated from most other students, he sensed some indefinable connection to them. His classmates thought of him as dull and humorless. He ignored them because there was always Mona. She thought the world of him and he could do nothing but reciprocate.

He met her in geology class, one of those elective courses he squeezed into his busy schedule. Mona was assigned to be his lab partner. They quickly became friends. Then they became more than friends. During geology field trips they collected and identified fossils, often laughing as they mispronounced the Latinized fossil names. He remembered their conversations after studying together at the library.

"Well, Mister Smart Alex, you sure messed up that last bunch! You still can't tell the difference between brachiopods and trilobites, can you?" she said teasing him. On field trips they followed a path along Scott's Run, a small stream whose dark brown earth embankment yielded those fossils he had difficulty in identifying. When they were out of sight of the others, she often casually took his hand. They even kissed once and he saw the golden hue of her hair enhanced by the sun's rays slipping through the trees.

"Give me time; I'm only a poor dimwitted engineer-to-be! What do I know? What can you expect from me?" Tobin chuckled, "You know I didn't have to take this course." That was true but he also knew that if he had not taken the course they might never have met.

"So, Tobin, are you still going to major in architecture?"

"That's what I planned to do, but I have to settle on just learning to be a plain old engineer." Indeed that's what he became, a civil engineer, fascinated by understanding why and how everything worked.

"What about you Mona, what do you plan to do with all that liberal arts stuff you are stuffing into your pretty head, huh?"

She grew serious and pensive for a few moments before flashing a wonderful smile.

"I love the theater and performing ... soooo . . . after graduation I'm going to try to get into Julliard or the Actor's Studio in New York. I would like to try to make it on stage if I can." He winced a bit, hoping she did not see him frown.

"Suppose you don't make it?"

"Then I'll just grab me one of those smart business majors around here who made lots of money, get hitched, and have a bunch of kids!" she explained, giggling all the while. Her laugh was endearing and Tobin would remember it forever.

As it turned out, she did attend both Julliard and the Actor's Studio. She didn't have to marry a money-making business major after all, Tobin thought. She went on to have a lucrative career on stage although most of her work was Off-Broadway and she supported herself by acting and doing voice-overs in commercials of all kinds. Tobin followed her career carefully until he himself was married. Then he forgot about Mona entirely, too busy with his job and his life.

He worked for the government doing analytical work sifting through pages of documents attempting to piece together information some of which was in published form or found in periodicals from all over the world. Then later he was sent to contact and interrogate agents, compiling information and bringing it back to the States. There were several 'arcs' and over time he flew to each as jet travel became common.

The 'central arc' involved stays in Zurich, Munich, Vienna and Budapest. The 'northern arc' found him visiting Prague, Berlin, Oslo, and Helsinki. He seldom traveled in the 'southern arc' that included Rome, Belgrade, Istanbul, and Baghdad. Others were covering the 'eastern arcs' somewhere in the Far East. Each of his visits took several days as there were many contacts at each, and that affected his marriage to Valerie who he met after leaving college. Valerie was a chief secretary in the department where he worked and later would become one of the finest women lawyers in the country. They were very much in love at first but Tobin's long and frequent absences changed all of that.

"Tobin, we need to talk," she said one evening. He sensed the subject she was about to broach. Those four words were foreboding and he waited quietly for her to continue.

"We're not growing younger, you know . . . but . . . frankly we are growing apart, too . . . too much if you ask me. You are gone almost three-quarters of the time flying around the world God knows where since I haven't handled any of your reports anymore since we married five years ago."

"I know I'm sorry but there isn't much I can do about that at this time . . . maybe later I can." She paused and he detected her hesitancy. She was frowning and tears began to well up in her eyes as she looked at him steadily. He waited some more.

"I've been seeing someone . . . someone you don't even know and it is becoming serious so I must ask for a divorce." Tobin stared at her. He was stunned but quickly found his composure realizing that she was right. His work was destroying their marriage. He must let her go. That happened some twenty years ago and now, semi-retired, he prepared to go to his college reunion

He visited the campus only once before and now was reluctant to go back there. But places intrigued him, especially those in which he spent time. Tobin was fascinated with what they contained. Each space to him possessed a form, and each was infused with some quality that lingered on. He visualized people and objects that once occupied them. Closing his eyes Tobin could see what had been there. This faculty was useful in his work, and now he visualized the old campus that Mona and he had shared long ago.

He recalled other experiences with spaces and his reactions, which were physical and emotional. He first became aware of their enchantment while visiting the house where he was born, a place he hadn't visited for years. Then a friend purchased it and invited Tobin over. An aura of previous times was discernable as he sauntered through the various rooms savoring glimpses of the past. Later he experienced those feelings when visiting the house where he lived as a youth. There he again sensed pleasant sensations of presences permeating the spaces. Later, after his former High School was turned into county offices, Tobin found himself paying property taxes in the room where industrial arts had been taught years before.

He had whittled away there on a lathe watching shavings fly from the revolving piece of wood clamped into the machine and drop gently to the floor. Returning to those places activated deep memories, sensations that captured his attention then and now. Occasionally that occurred when he simply thought of spaces he had once known. Tobin's reflections were a stream of heightened déjà vu, a powerful connection with past and present merging within his body and his mind.

Sitting at his desk now he tried visualizing his old classmates. They were probably much older. Were they wiser? Had they accomplished what they set out to do? Surely they have expanded the narrow beliefs and ideas of their youth. We've all taken separate paths, and have done different things. Seeing them again might be interesting. And what was campus like now? Tobin smiled while writing his check to register for the reunion. Several days later he received a list of his classmates still living, and another of those planning to attend. He recognized a few names from each. He shrugged as he contemplated the weekend ahead deciding that he would not expect much and thus avoid disappointment.

"Oh, what the hell! It's just a weekend. I surely can handle that." When the day arrived to leave, Tobin packed a small bag and tossed it into his car. Driving to the small town in the other end of the state would be quicker on the interstate highway that did not exist before, but Tobin chose to follow the old highways along which he often stood hitchhiking at street corners in towns along the way. He recognized some. Others had changed but he knew when he passed them by his sensations.

The university and the small town that surrounded it had grown. Some of the stores on Main Street had changed. Some were modernized. Others aged gracelessly, now looking shabby and gray. There were several pizza parlors and fast food places that were non-existent before. Tobin drove through town and circled back parking near what had been one the favored drinking spots, the Top Notch. It was still there. He sat on a stool at the small bar sipping a glass of beer.

The room was the same, blessed with the semi-darkness which had given more ordinary looking coeds a fair chance with the male students. Now during the middle of the day, and with most of the students gone for the summer only a few people sat in the booths along the wall. They appeared to be older and probably were some members of his class that he did not recognize. As Tobin sensed pleasant vibrations of days long gone, he heard a familiar voice call his name.

"Toby, Goddammit, is that you?" A tall man with a slight paunch rose from one of the booths and ambled over to where Tobin sat at the bar, slapping him on the back.

"Son of a bitch . . . it is you!" exclaimed the stranger

"Do I know you?" Tobin mockingly responded.

"You old bastard, you sure as hell should! I'm Marty!" said a raspy voice responding to Tobin's feigned blank stare which morphed into a wide grin. The voice continued, "Martin Sloan! Take a closer look, remember me now? We shared some of those boring classes in Gadsden Hall. There was that lousy psyche class . . . and labor econ and Dexter's history class," he laughed while speaking excitedly as if what he was saying would not be absorbed unless he hurried through his speech.

"I'll be damned, you don't look at all like the Marty I knew, but then you've changed quite a bit! . . . How are you, Marty?"

"Great. . . been making tons of money! Divorced three times! The first died on me, the second took me to the cleaners, but I soon made up for it. Now I'm just a rich lonely old fart who flies off to Jamaica every winter to play golf until I hit all the goddamn balls into the ocean!"

Tobin lived a modest life. He too lost a wife, and considered himself an old fart, but he never thought of himself as lonely. As a matter of fact one of the reasons he delayed in making up his mind to come to the reunion was that he was busy writing, a passion that recently appeared. Besides his former classmates were all probably rich and he certainly wasn't. He sent only a small contribution to the alumni association.

"Sent them a goddamned ton of dough!" blurted Martin, "Hey, I got a room at the Campus Inn. Where you staying?"

"Same place."

"Great! Maybe we can go to some of the events together if my fraternity brothers will let me hang out with a god damned independent!" Tobin had shunned fraternity life.

They finished their beer. Martin stayed for more, but Tobin hurried away wanting to look over the campus. He checked in at the Inn and then walked through the campus. Newer buildings sprouted up in each direction. Several new dormitories stood like sentinels surrounding classroom buildings, each blending with the architectural Williamsburg style still favored by university trustees. Soon he found himself in the middle of what had been the center of the campus. Closing his eyes he saw streams of students pouring out of each classroom building.

His mind's eye filled with the sea of faces and bodies of students hurrying to classes. Pleasant memories surfaced, mingled with sadness. He opened his eyes and saw that he was practically alone. Only a few people were strolling along the sidewalk that sliced through the quadrangle. He savored the strong connection with the space while sauntering along 'slant walk' which cut diagonally through the center of campus. It was quiet and serene. The scene with people in his mind was gone.

A door to Gadsden Hall where Tobin studied calculus, advanced mathematics, and history was open. He pushed through into silence. The building was empty. The only sounds were his own footsteps clomping down the hall. He poked his head into a classroom. Familiar wooden seats had been replaced with cold plastic chairs. Blackboards now were green-boards. Everything was different and yet the same. Smells and sensations intensified. In the room where

Professor Dexter held court, he could almost hear him saying that understanding the past would help us understand both the present and future.

Tobin paused for several minutes for no particular reason enjoying the moment. He strolled through Pearson Hall where he studied Labor Economics, literature courses, and French. Leaving it, he entered the library. The sun's rays streaked through the windows of the dome above the lobby, casting flickering shadows on the granite floor below. No one was here either. That was fine with Tobin who knew that he couldn't explain what he was experiencing to anyone.

For a moment he thought Mona was sitting at that long table in the library where they shared their studies. She understood his affinity to spaces. He wondered if others experienced the subtle joy in being alive in a place they previously had occupied. He wondered if he could describe it if someone asked. Fool, he thought, the poets have already done that far above my poor powers to add or detract. The use of Lincoln's words amused him. He chuckled quietly and left the building.

He strolled 'up' slant walk, stopping where an old stone fountain made by a retired mason had been replaced by a newer version in brick. Its cold concrete benches contrasted with the vision in Tobin's memory. My God, even the new fountain is made in Williamsburg style. The rustic old fountain had been a meeting place for students, and he met Mona there many times on their way to the library to study. Probably students met there during the school year. Now it stood empty, just vacant space.

Tobin continued through a brick archway at the corner where the campus melded into town. He wandered past the book stores, both of which had moved to larger quarters across the street where Pete's coffee shop once stood. It was gone. It was there where he and a few iconoclastic comrades sipped java, smoked endless cigarettes, plunked quarters into the juke box and argued about the Korean War. He turned and headed toward The Inn walking past the president's house. There was a new president now. The house looked the same. The president he remembered now occupied space in the cemetery.

Tobin took a nap before leaving for the Student Union where dinner and reunion ceremonies were scheduled. He was late. Hoping to avoid Martin Sloan, he found a seat at one of the round banquet tables at the rear of the large room filled with graduates from several classes. Others at the table greeted him warmly. He was surprised by their friendliness but did not remember any of them. There was one vacant chair, but alas, Martin soon appropriated it. He began regaling his captive audience with his adventures in the world of business. Modesty was not one of his characteristics, but Tobin was certain that much of Marty's bragging had basis in fact. Marty had always been a savvy and ruthless player.

There are probably many reasons for attending this gathering of strangers, Tobin thought. A few perhaps, like Martin, came to gloat over their success in whatever ventures they pursued during the years just passed. Others simply came to enjoy a nostalgic weekend similar to what Tobin anticipated. Perhaps both the ego and the soul of each person attending the event were nourished somehow in ways unknown even to themselves.

Dinner was served along with small talk. Several of those around the table were reluctant to talk of their accomplishments and required some coaxing. Martin was not one of them. Most of the others spoke of children and grandchildren through whom they perceived a sense of immortality. All had been successful in various ventures. Sitting at the table along with their spouses were classmates who represented a variety of vocations; there was a financial adviser, a banker, two teachers, a physicist, and a physician. Only one woman was a member of the class, and her husband had attended another university and sat quietly next to her. But Martin always liked to stir things up. Fortunately the meal had ended and speeches had not begun.

"The government's gotten too big," declared Marty, who chose to break the rule against discussing politics or religion at social gatherings. Everyone at the table except Tobin seemed to shared Marty's political views, which he expounded upon at length and encouraged other to join in.

"We've got to get rid of all these welfare idlers," someone quickly added, "They just increase our taxes, cost us more and for what?"

"And they contribute nothing to the economy."

"Or society!" Everyone laughed.

"They stifle it!"

"Which?"

"Both!"

"Taxes are detrimental. They deter investments and kill off free competition and free enterprise," chimed another. Martin spurred on by this approbation digressed long enough to describe how Tobin earned his reputation of being a dullard during their under-graduate days. But he waxed eloquent when speaking of his own independence, his hatred of government and the rules it imposed. Government had no business restricting his freedom to make more money.

"People have got to be independent like me," he said, "even a guy like Toby. But he always had his head in some book, even those that weren't required reading for any of our classes." It was true. Some unseen force seemed to compel Tobin then as now and he was always reading a book. While the others talked he sat quietly thinking about life's complexity and its many connections. There were multitudes of trivial and significant relationships connecting things and ideas.

Particles did their symbiotic dance and everything - stones, rock, earth, people, and the various parts of the universe reflect structure as numerous impressions filled minds connecting in many ways. Thought is born. And that spawns the creativity that fueled innovation and the arts that generated great poetry, and the literature extolling life and its virtues. Tobin ignored Martin's argument and rose from the table when dinner ended. Names of the more famous graduates were announced by the VIPs at the front table and each was met with applause as the graduate named rose to accept his or her accolades.

The people at Tobin's table continued listening to Martin's harangue while those at other tables stood in small clusters chatting amiably. Tobin saw someone he knew and walked over to speak with Nora and her husband. They shook hands and spoke briefly. Then he saw her. Mona was sitting by herself at a table against the wall. He walked quickly over to her.

"Mona! Is that really you?"

"Tobin! My God, it's good to see you!"

"Why didn't they introduce you as the celebrity you are?"

"I didn't use my stage name."

"Why not? I've been following your career for years." She laughed and Tobin sensed the past as well as the present.

"What's have you been doing with your life, Tobin?" He told of working for the government but skipped all the details.

". . .and besides that I've had a marriage go sour on me."

"Don't fret my boy! I've been through three of them. Never marry in the theater. One was a producer, one was a director and one an actor. Mingling egos is terribly damaging to marriage!" They exchanged other information and laughed together the rest of the evening, enjoying the dance that followed dinner.

"I arrived quite late," she said, "And I do want to walk around and see the campus during daytime, especially those places where we used to hang out. Remember? Will you take me for a walk around tomorrow, Tobin?"

"Sure, I'd love to," he did not tell her that he had already taken his tour of the places and planned to leave early in the morning. But plans are made to be changed.

"After walking around the campus I want to hike out along Scott's Run for a little while, okay?"

"Why on earth would you want to do that?"

"I just want to see if after all these years you can tell the difference between brachiopods and trilobites!" She smiled and her eyes twinkled. Tobin saw that she was more attractive than he had remembered. He smiled as she reached over and touched his hand

"Okay, it's a date!"

Sanctuary

THE MEN CAME FROM various villages scattered throughout the countryside. Some came farther than others, walking for hours before boarding the hot dusty bus that brought them to this place. There were almost two dozen of them. They wore ragged clothing and looked weather-beaten and sad. Their aim was to cross the river into that other country, find work, and make money to send back to their families. Eventually they would return to be with them, or if possible bring them over into that other country as well. Among them was an older man whose name was Carlos Gabrielo.

"Carlos, they tell me you have crossed over many times, why did you not stay then?"

"Listen, Chiquita, I love my own country better but there is no work here. I went for the bucks that's all, and when I made a bunch I brought it back here for my family. Now I go out of habit, I dunno, it's something I feel I need to do." In truth, Carlos did not wish to reveal his feelings whatever they were. Desperate men do desperate things. He knew the way and all that he wanted to do was get them all across safely.

"Can you get us over there tonight?" asked another.

"Hell yes, I've done it many times, but I insist that you follow my directions to the hilt or else you will not make it."

"We'll do whatever you say, Carlos!"

"Yes, Carlos, we'll do as you say."

They walked slowly for over a mile smoking cigarettes and talking softly among themselves in the dark before reaching the river bank. They could hear the water flowing softly even before they saw it shining in the half-moon light. Carlos led them along a narrow path to a place where he called them together. They listened to his instructions before stripping to their shorts and placing their clothes into plastic bags. Carlos led the way as they entered the river at one of its narrowest points where it was possible for them to swim across despite any current. They waded as far as they could and when their feet no longer touched bottom, they began swimming, holding their plastic bags above their heads as they formed a long line stretching almost a third of the way across.

Across the river a man had been watching them with great interest. He sat on a large bolder with a high-powered rifle lying across his lap, the kind of weapon used to hunt game. There was enough light from the moon which occasionally slid behind clouds for the man to make out the moving forms of the swimmers. He snubbed out the cigarette he was smoking and slowly lifted the rifle to his shoulder. He took careful aim at the first man in the line and squeezed the trigger three times. Three small steel missiles raced toward their target as the roar of the rifle shots reverberated through the still night, its sound echoing from the river bank and swallowed by the trees.

The men following Carlos panicked. They turned and swam or waded quickly back to the shore they had just left. One man's body floated slowly downstream. It was Carlos. The man got off his perch on the bolder and walked a short distance to a dirty pickup truck and drove away without a word and without remorse. The frightened swimmers dashed madly away from the river. But a few of them stopped to look back. Gesturing to each other, three of them turned and walked half-crouched back to the rivers edge. When the body floated near enough to the shore one of the men waded out and grabbed it. It was still clutching a plastic bag. He pulled it closer to shore and the other two men stepped into the river helping him pull Carlos from the water. Then one of them stumbled along the narrow path to summon the others who were shivering with fear, reluctant to respond and crouching with wide eyes holding the look of terror. But a few of them quietly crept back to view the body.

"Poor son of a bitch, he didn't know what hit him, did he?""No," another man said, "At least he didn't feel a thing."

"Let's get the hell out of here!"

"Yes, the bastard that did this may still be watching!"

One of the men knew the town Carlos came from and they decided to take his body there. Some of the other men wandered away while four others carried the lifeless body. Upon reaching the small village where they had rendezvoused just a few hours before they found a man with a small truck who agreed to drive them and Carlos home for a few cigarettes. The four men who accompanied the body sat in silence all through the bouncy trip smoking cigarettes and quietly contemplating whether or not to attempt a crossing later that evening or wait until tomorrow. Their families were near starvation. They had to go. They must find jobs. They would try again despite what had happened.

They took Carlos' body to the church where his oldest son, Sebastian, had been priest for a short time. Sebastian had chosen to attend the seminary because it was the only way for him to obtain an education. While there he also studied agriculture. He always loved the soil and as a child played in it by making small roads for his toy automobile, which he maneuvered over them with childish glee. Normally a new priest was not assigned to the parish where he had lived but since no other priest could be found for his home town, Sebastian was sent.

A mortician was called to prepare the body for burial. There were three ugly wounds where the bullets ripped into the head, the chest and the left shoulder. Carlos' wife died several years before, but three of his other children lived in nearby villages. If the death of his father wasn't enough, everything had changed for Sebastian while hearing confessions just a few hours before. He listened patiently and absolved the sins of several others before a young man entered.

"Bless me Father for I have sinned," said a nervous voice.

"What is your sin my son?"

The man was distraught and spoke hesitantly, pausing often to gasp for breath which seemed to come only with some difficulty. His guilt-ridden and tremulous voice rose at times and faded into a hoarse whisper at others.

"I couldn't help it! . . . I was provoked! . . . Maria and I had been together that way . . . for some time . . . but then Antonio, he's the one . . . Antonio came between us . . . last night at the cantina we argued about it . . . he and I . . . about Maria . . . I would have been alright except that I drank too much and then she laughed at me . . . and Antonio spit at me and called me names . . . that did it . . . I went into a rage . . . Antonio and I fought and I was winning until he pulled a knife . . . I wrestled it away from him and before I knew . . .it. . . plunged into him . . . not once but several times . . .tears ran down my face for we had been friends for years . . . oh my God, what have I done? . . . he died this morning . . . the police are looking for me!" Sebastian was stunned and for a few moments couldn't find the words he needed to say.

"Make a good act of contrition now my son and then for your penance say ten Our Father's and ten Hail Mary's." He paused as the mixed feelings of horror and repulsion could be felt in his body. He spoke the next few words with authority. "That is what you owe to God . . . and you must of course surrender yourself to the police and pay the civil penalty for your crime for that is what you owe to the state."

"Thank you, Father." Sebastian sat frozen for a long moment. He had recognized the supplicant's voice immediately. It was that of his younger brother, Ernesto who was quick tempered and impulsive like their father. It was just an hour later after leaving the confessional that Sebastian was informed of his father's death. His burden of sorrow had doubled in a very short period of time. Now he began to make arrangements for one funeral knowing that there would be another soon after. He called the Bishop on the telephone for permission to bury his father.

"Carlos Gabrielo cannot be given the Mass of the Christian Burial!" declared the bishop in a voice that sounded more angry and less compassionate, "Nor can his body be buried in the sanctified ground of the Church Cemetery!"

"Why in God's name not?" asked Sebastian, "I wish to do the Mass for him . . . he was my father after all!"

"Carlos Garbielo stopped attending Sunday Mass long ago, and has not received the Sacraments for years . . . ever since his wife died. Then we had words. He cursed both me and God, and then continued to blaspheme the Church as well!"

"What does that mean? That means nothing! He was always an angry man trying to feed his family! He worked hard all his life and was full of love for his family and for his friends." He paused, "And he loved God, too. That I know, and that I can and will attest to!"

"Then tell me why he was going to cross the river again! That is always a dangerous thing to do. His children are grown, they are making their way alone. It was his anger at me and God that took him to the river last night, and it was his anger toward me and toward God that killed him!"

Sebastian listened to the Bishop's last words in obedient but angry silence. He could not believe what he was hearing. Where was the compassion of Christ in all of this? He started to protest, but the bishop was adamant and Sebastian was obliged to heed his instructions. He sat quietly holding onto the telephone for several minutes until his anger subsided. He knew that he could not change the bishop's mind whose position denied Carlos not only the Mass but also burial beside his wife. Sebastian had only himself been a priest for a short time, but he was extremely upset by the turn of events. He had gone to the seminary because of his thirst for knowledge and his plan was to be a priest while helping poor farmers with newer methods of planting and fertilization.

The next day with his siblings and a few men from the village, they took the body from the mortician. Just beyond the village there was a small area not fit for much of anything. It was the burial place for criminals, suicides, and those who had not received baptism from the Church. A few boxes became a makeshift altar upon which Sebastian said the funeral Mass. He stayed behind after the others left, sitting in silence on the ground next to Carlos Gabrielo's grave. He had no more prayers to say and just sat there staring at the mound of earth for a long time. Finally he rose and walked slowly away.

The next day, Ernesto was tried and convicted of murdering Antonio. The trial did not take long because Ernesto, filled with remorse, readily admitted to the killing. Maria Valdez sat sobbing all through the trial as her one lover was sentenced for the death of the other. Now she was sad and lonely. Her ambivalence had set the two friends at each other and one was dead and the other soon would be. Ernesto's execution would take place immediately since the local jail could not afford to feed a condemned man any more than it already had. Sebastian stood nearby praying while Ernesto smoked a last cigarette.

"Pray for me brother . . . I mean, Father! I really didn't mean to kill Antonio! I am sorry and . . . please tell God that! Oh, I loved Maria so much! And I brought shame upon the family name and now I will join our poor father who waits in heaven!" A soldier tied a blindfold over Ernesto's eyes and stepped away.

"I will Ernesto, I will!" Sebastian closed his eyes, "Kyrie eleison, Christe eleision, Kyrie eleison," then after a short pause, "Domine, animam ejus, requiescat in pace!" Again rifle shots echoed, but this time against the wall of the small jailhouse. Again a small procession formed taking Ernesto's body to that small graveyard for criminals, suicides, and those who had not been baptized.

The following day Sebastian gave what money he had to his sisters. They did not attend the execution because their husbands forbade them from doing so. Sebastian did not stay in town very long. He left a short note for the Bishop on the altar of the little church that he loved. Then he took the bus to the capitol where he went to see a friend who had been with him at the seminary and now worked for the government. The friend looked up with surprise when Sebastian walked into his office.

"My friend, Sebastian! What are you doing here?"

"I need a visa so I can cross the river."

"And just what do you plan to do there, my friend?"

"I will work . . . I will go to school . . . a university."

"Where?"

"At any one that will allow me. I need to learn more, I need to do more. I cannot stay here any longer."

"What about the Church?"

"You left the seminary, why can't I leave the priesthood?"

"But I am an agnostic. You . . . you are a believer!"

"I'm no longer certain of that . . . I don't know." He told of his father's death and his brother's execution, the Bishop's denial of Christian burial for both while his agnostic friend listened to him quietly. A visa for Sebastian was obtained in a few days, and he crossed the river. He dropped the "o" from his last name and removed the collar of a priest from around his neck. He could no longer be one. He made his way to a university in a large city in a mid-western state where he began his studies while working part-time as a waiter. It was a restaurant frequented by professors and instructors from the university.

"You're new here, aren't you?" one of them asked him one day when Sebastian brought a meal to the tall man sitting alone.

"Yes, I am."

"However you look familiar to me."

"I am in your history class, Professor Dexter!"

"Oh, yes, you're the one with one degree and now are working on another. That's very good. Do you plan to teach? The college needs graduate instructors, you know, especially now."

"You are very kind, Professor, but my field is agronomy and not the classics or history or literature. I want to help those who till the soil and grow the food we eat."

"That is fine, but you must know that every field offers opportunities to teach as well as to learn. Your field is also essential to life, perhaps even more so than mine." Dexter said. "Do consider giving it a try."

"Thank you, sir, but my English is not the best."

"It will only get better, my friend."

While there were thousands attending the university there were very few Hispanic students and the push for faculty diversity provided Sebastian with an opportunity to teach. He become a lecturer, finishing his master's degree the following spring and quickly began work toward his doctorate.

Sebastian was a diligent student and over time developed fluency in three languages. He adapted rapidly as each door of opportunity opened for him and he continued with an indomitable appetite for learning. His knowledge in his field increased dramatically. Eventually he became noted for his expertise and later when Aaron Dexter moved to a small town, Sebastian joined him and taught at the same university. He grew to enjoy living in a small town. It reminded him of his former home.

Terra Incognita

THE BUSINESS WORLD PROVED to be a perfect match for Martin Sloan. It became a world that he knew very well and one which he soon mastered. Not only did he thrive, but he carved out a comfortable existence for himself. After finishing his tour of duty with the Air Force, he obtained his MBA and left college to work diligently for one of those huge corporations, first in middle management before moving rapidly into upper levels until he realized that he could do better on his own. And he did. What spurred him on to that accomplishment was a woman.

It was the last straw when his company promoted a woman to head the firm he worked for. Sloan had known Nora Madison during his university days. They were in several classes together including a course taught by her father. It was obvious to Martin if not to everyone else that Nora's success was due to her good looks and her many connections. But his envy blinded him to the fact that she was a highly capable executive and that he also was quite willing to use connections and manipulate others whenever such activities furthered his career. However his bruised ego pushed him into even more successful ventures than he could ever have imagined.

After resigning from the corporation, Martin soon established himself as a power broker of sorts. What followed was a series of financial successes. Every venture he organized led to an even more successful one. He epitomized the Midas touch. Although extra-marital affairs that he sometimes failed to keep hidden cost him huge sums of money, he had by then accumulated more money than he knew what to do with anyway. In his 'mental accounting' he simply wrote off his philandering incursions as simply experiences that a man of great means could afford. And he was not reluctant to take credit for his conquests both in the board room and the bedroom. Another opportunity for him to boast of his success came during the reunion of his college graduating class at the university.

He took full advantage of captive audiences at his old fraternity and later at the reunion dinner, which he left somewhat perturbed over remarks made by someone who he thought of as a friend. Martin had been too absorbed in himself and his own interpretations of society and politics while failing to listen and comprehend what Tobin had said. Martin was also angry at himself for not marshalling more succinct arguments. But his other failing was that he did not wish to examine or understand ideas and concepts that challenged his beliefs. He simply refused to consider them. He had always been single-minded, something that worked quite well for him in the business world. Success for him was a bankroll and whatever status it produced. And Martin was not really such a bad person. He lived in a manner to which he became accustomed. Foremost in his mind was having his way regardless of what others thought, what others may feel, and what others may want or need.

Following the class reunion, Martin took a taxi to a nearby airport after breakfast the next morning. There he boarded his private jet and soon was lost in his thoughts and the puffy white clouds that the speeding aircraft sliced through. Martin had sat with Tobin at breakfast where he had an opportunity to listen to his former classmate but instead took charge as usual.

"Whatever the hell you are into, Toby, give it up and come join my company. You can have a private jet too, if you like! I always need a good man . . . someone I can trust." He recalled that several former employees had to be dismissed because of tendencies to take what was not theirs, a habit which they may have learned by observing the attitudes and manners of their employer. Martin was not above using underhanded tactics when he thought them essential to reach his goals. Ethics for him was something other guys should follow and he could ignore if the situation warranted. Tobin smiled and said nothing while sipping his coffee.

"Just where the hell are you working now. You haven't said much about that during our stay on campus?" forgetting that he had monopolized every conversation that they had.

"I think I did mention that I worked for the government, but probably you didn't hear me." Tobin was not able to disclose exactly what his work entailed because much of it had to do with classified material. His job was highly sensitive and required not only secrecy but also a great deal of thought and analysis.

"God that must be one hell-hole to work in, huh? I mean all those damned bureaucrats and crooked politicians. Politicians, hell . . . I buy them by the dozen just to keep government off my back! So tell me, what is it that you do and how much do they pay you to do it? I'll double that . . . wait, make that triple that!"

"Someone has to regulate you tycoons before you steal the public and each other blind," responded Tobin with a wide grin but not saying much more.

"And what is it exactly that you do, Toby?"

"The work centers mostly on gathering and analyzing information of all kinds from a variety of places and circumstances, much coming from foreign sources and then I regularly report to those needing such information."

"You aren't a spy are you?" aid Martin scrutinizing Tobin and expecting to grasp whatever it was he was doing.

Tobin said nothing but simply smiled and sat there looking pleasant, a useful attitude when dealing with people like Martin, people who were aggressive and domineering. After obtaining his bachelor's degree Martin served in the Air Force as a fighter pilot flying sorties over North Korea during the war. He would gladly have crossed the Yalu River into China and bombed and strafed the hell out of them if he would have gotten the go-ahead, Goddamned Communists didn't deserve to live. He was a very good pilot and looked down upon the 'poor bastards in the infantry' as fools, 'ground-pounders.' He knew he was better than them. Now he was miffed. Tobin would not work for him saying that he could not work with him, whatever the hell that meant. Ah hell, Toby was always an enigma anyway.

The jet made a soft landing at an air strip a few miles from Martin's home. He climbed into a waiting sedan, a high powered Mercedes parked in the hangar and drove off with a roar. Rain fell softly at first but then it increased, eventually coming down in torrents. Martin had difficulty seeing the winding road and he drove as aggressively as he had flown as a fighter pilot, as he did everything else. But now something clouded his mind. Tobin's way of thinking annoyed him. What bothered him most was that he was unable to manipulate Toby and affect his weird thinking. That's it . . . sure . . . listening to that goddamned fool had messed up my head. His concentration on driving diminished as anger increased, and he was unaware of the turn in the road.

He lost control of the Mercedes. It began sliding first to the left and then to the right before moving sideways across both lanes of the road. Fortunately there was no other traffic and Martin gunned the motor trying to control the careening auto without success. It left the road and going airborne it tumbled end over end down an embankment before righting itself and then rolling several times, bouncing its way to the bottom of a deep ravine coming to rest upright in a shallow stream a few hundred feet below the roadway. The rear of the Mercedes was partially submerged. The last things Martin heard was screeching metal followed by water bubbling underneath him and the car. Then he lost consciousness.

The airbags activated. Despite them his seat belt broke and Martin was tossed around and badly injured on the rapid descent that tore a path through brush decapitating several small trees on the way down. Martin and his Mercedes would have remained unnoticed except that the driver following Martin's car saw it leave the road and summoned police and emergency people. They arrived on the scene within twenty-five minutes and two of the rescue crew tossed lines into the ravine on which they rappelled to the battered half submerged Mercedes.

"Anybody in it?" asked one.

"Just one guy," said the man who broke a window and reached inside feeling Martin's pulse. His companion signaled to others above for tools to cut open the wreckage. Another twenty minutes went by before they got Martin out and up to the ambulance waiting above. He was now in a strange place, an unknown world, the terra incognita of delirium. In his mind Martin crawled desperately through what seemed like a large endless tunnel. There was a strong light somewhere shining in his eyes, but eventually he found himself in a wide opening filled with people. At first they all looked to be strangers until Martin became aware that they were people he had known at different times during his life. Many of them were people who he had stepped on during his meteoric ascent as a tycoon.

The large group of people formed a line that snaked its way toward a large gate up ahead. Martin never could stand lines and charged past everyone while none of them complained about his overbearing manner. They stood silently. He ignored them, throwing vitriolic curses until he came upon a strange looking fellow near what appeared to be the gate.

"What is this place?" Martin asked. The stern looking man at the gate resembled Tobin and simply stared at him in disbelief, saying nothing, but shaking his head. "Am I dead, or what?" Martin demanded to know while fully expecting answers. There were none and Martin again found himself in the tunnel clawing his way forward on his hands and knees. What the hell is going on, he thought. A strange series of images appeared. They moved past slowly. He stopped to look. At first he did not recognize what he was seeing. Then it dawned on him that much of what he had done in the past had caused pain and suffering for many people. Those people were here, in line, staring at him now.

What disturbed him was that now he actually cared for those people whereas before he had always remained aloof with his intimidating manner and haughty indifference. He observed infractions he had committed, hurts he had inflicted. Martin for the first time in his life experienced a bitter feeling, a deep sense of remorse. It was like watching a bad movie. Martin stared at the endless procession of his previous activities, more sad than terror stricken. He was a man not easily frightened, but these scenes were more than he could stomach. He closed his eyes and wanted all of it to end. He wanted to die. Then another light appeared somewhere in the distance yet close.

"Mister Sloan, can you hear me?" said a pleasant voice.

Martin had lain in an intensive care unit for forty-seven hours after undergoing extensive surgery repairing his torn and shattered body. Punctured vital organs had been repaired and healing begun. A monitor suspended above his head displayed his vital signs. The day had gone by and another one was almost over when he heard that voice speaking to him reassuringly.

"You are going to be alright Mr. Sloan." It was dark in the room and the voice belonged to a nurse sitting nearby. She rose and leaned over Martin with her flashlight, "You can't talk now because of the ventilator, but you are doing fine. You probably want a drink of water but you can't swallow, so I'll wipe your lips with a sponge . . . try to sleep some more and you'll feel better in the morning."

Martin dosed off, experiencing bits of consciousness that contrasted with various dreams. Ever so slowly he began to understand something that had eluded him all his life. It was as if his brain had opened up and had absorbed information that he somehow missed along the way. He realized that it had been a nurse talking to him and not the stranger resembling Tobin. He tried to think about what had happened but much of that had disappeared from his mind. His memory seemed to grab only small pieces. Complete memory would return later.

Strange thoughts occurred to him. Questions appeared. But now where was he morphed into who was he? Martin grew more aware of life despite the mental haze induced by pain killing medication. He was astounded by the clarity of what he could see now that he awoke in a dark room. For the first time in his life he was truly conscious. He had been in an unknown land but now he was awake. Yes, he would be fine. And yes, there were several things that he needed and wanted to do and none of them concerned the making of more money.

Ubiquity

Like falling leaves
Or tumbling snowflakes
Truly you and I are
Wind driven falling pell-mell
Falsely believing control
And direction is always ours.

Through tumultuous times
Filled with joys and sorrows
Between inertia and action
Suffering anticipations
Enduring expectations
Leaving only memory.

The clear summons beckons
For some but a faint whisper
While for others almost all
It is unheard non-existent
Or ignored like the unseen
Beauty reality lurking hidden
Behind under the earthly fog
In which we live.

Victor

IT WAS TRULY A grand wedding. Almost everybody in town attended. Some came to gawk. Some came to talk. Even a rich uncle of the bride's mother, Pietro Marfido, from the old country came. There had always been talk that Estelle Valrico would never catch a man because she was ungainly as a young girl and everyone thought she would remain that way forever. During her childhood and early youth Estelle was a Tomboy, preferring rough-house play with boys to playing with dolls. Everyone called her Stella at high school. During those days she grew tall with long legs that held a firm and delightfully formed body. And she grew more attractive with each passing year.

While playing with the 'guys,' the ideas of sexual encounters never crossed her mind until she experienced unusual sensations at the age of fifteen when wrestling with one of them in the park, and although she liked Ernie because he was cute and Joey because he was smart, Dominic was her favorite. He was the best athlete, strong and nimble. It was during the time he wrestled her to the ground and rolled over her that the sensations appeared for the first time within her. When others called him to play baseball, Dominic quickly jumped up and raced off leaving her on the ground with a mysterious, but pleasant desire.

"See you later, Esther! He yelled as he ran away.

"That's not my name!" she yelled angrily at him. He stopped and turned to yell back, "Esther means 'Star,'" and so does Stella. You ought to know that by now!"

"What do you know, smart aleck!" she yelled back.

Stella sat in the grass after this exchange trying to hold back the tears streaming down her cheeks until after Dominic was out of sight. Her tears were not from sadness or pain. No, none of that. The wonder of her experience overwhelmed her and she worried about those strange sensations and her new found awareness of them. Curiosity led her to ask the few girl friends she knew about the experience. She knew her mother would frown upon discussing such things with her. But the female friends offered little help. They mostly giggled as she related her experience to them, but they did admit to having occasionally induced something like those pleasant sensations she had felt. Later Stella tried that, but found it lacking the intensity she experienced while with Dominic.

A few years later Stella Valrico graduated from high school with honors and like many others went off to college unsure of what she wanted to do with her life. Dominic, who was a year or two older had already gone to another college and was but a fading memory. But changes came rapidly for Stella over the next few years. She was now an extremely attractive woman. Then her appearance became a handicap as she discovered that most boys only wanted to sleep with her. Friendship or romance was not their agenda. Other boys that she wanted to meet and get to know were awed by her beauty, afraid to approach her. She was a virgin when she graduated from college and felt somehow cheated, certain she was missing out on something, but took solace in the fact that she wasn't alone.

Stella took a teaching job in the city. She also did part-time modeling for catalogs and brochures and quickly learned which postures were required and how to do them well. She grew aware of her sexual appeal and became aware that men were easily aroused by visual stimulation. Modeling paid well while modeling nude paid better. She seldom visited her home town or her family. The first time was to comfort her mother when her father, Joseph Valrico died unexpectedly of a heart attack. The next time she returned home she brought with her a surprise. She announced that she was getting married. Her small town friends and acquaintances pried her with dozens of questions.

"What's he like, Stel?"

"Is he rich?"

"Is he good looking?"

"Is there going to be a wedding shower we can come to?"

"Where'd you meet him?"

"Have you done it with him yet?"

"Look! She's blushing, she did! . . . She did it!"

"I'll bet you're getting real excited, huh?"

"Are you getting married at Saint Ed's?"

Stella had broken the news to her mother in advance over the telephone. She arrived a few days later with her fiancé and introduced him to everyone.

"Mama, this is Martin Sloan." Later when she and her mother were alone Stella told her how they met at a party several months ago. Although he was twenty years older, she was taken by his charm and manners. It didn't hurt that he had loads of money. Stella knew that he had been divorced ten years before, and there would be one complication. Stella was raised a Catholic and Martin was Jewish, but since neither practiced their religions to any degree, their outdoor wedding would be presided over by a Methodist minister.

Her mother was not pleased about that and made her feelings known to Stella but to no avail. However, the rich uncle from the old country got along well with Martin. Pietro Marfido seemed to be the only one. They talked a good deal about stocks and bonds. The wedding turned out to be the most splendid the townsfolk had ever witnessed. Almost everybody in town it seems was invited. If they hadn't been invited they simply showed up and joined the curious crowd of people whose eyes followed the bride and the groom with envy. Tongues wagged.

"He's Jewish, you know!"

"Who'd a thunk Estelle would marry a Jew!"

"Don't worry, it won't last long"

"How do you know that, blabbermouth?"

"They say he's thirty years older than her."

"And divorced twice, don't forget that!"

"No, one of them died."

"So they say!"

"At least he's got lots of money."

"Did you taste the champagne? It's really good!"

"I'll give them about two years!"

"I'll bet she's knocked up already."

After the lavish feast, Stella and Martin flew away in a chartered jet to honeymoon in Hawaii. Upon their return Martin surprised her with a newly built house that he recently purchased. It was a small mansion just outside the city where Martin lived and he gave up an apartment just as lavish. Things went well for the first year. That was because Martin was away a great deal of the time 'taking care of business.' Stella often found herself spending solitary hours browsing at the art museum or attending concerts alone. On those occasions when it was planned that Martin would accompany her to such events, he often telephoned his regrets telling her to go ahead without him because he could not make it in time. Business, you know. His priority.

Things also went badly in the bedroom. That did not please either of them. Stella was confused and disappointed. She had a few affairs prior to their marriage and now expected much more from a husband than what a lover could offer. She remembered those wonderful sensations when wrestling with Dominic. Even her lovers could not perform in a way that made her feel that way, the wonderful ecstasy she craved. She was saddened to learn that Dominic had been killed in Korea, and more saddened to see that her marriage was failing.

Often she blamed herself for not being able to arouse Martin sufficiently. She had no way of knowing that Martin was impotent and that he was only able to perform sexually while in the company of high-priced call-girls. That was something he kept secret from her along with another apartment on the other side of town he maintained for his clandestine liaisons. The few nights he spent at home began pleasantly but soon they were bickering and quarreling over trivialities. Both grew more miserable each day. Martin's absences grew longer. Stella grew lonely and desperate, even contemplating suicide more than once.

After several weeks of trying to make their marriage work, begging him to go with her for counseling, Stella gave up on Martin and her marriage. She packed up and moved out. There was a pre-nuptial agreement and Stella would receive little of the great wealth that Martin accumulated during their time together. But Stella didn't want money. She wanted love, the love she felt cheated of and those heavenly sensations she had experienced once a long time ago.

She returned to teaching and part-time modeling for a few years but found both unsatisfying. As time passed, she found there were fewer modeling jobs. The days and months and years disappeared. Finding work that paid well became difficult and Stella went to work as a night-club dancer which morphed into a better paying job. She became a stripper. Gradually her new way of life brought with it a sense of guilt that turned into a nagging depression. That grew unbearable. One of her friends at the club where she performed offered her something,

"Here honey, take this and you'll feel better right away and you won't be crying so much here in the dressing room, Jesus, you're making us all feel rotten!"

"What are these pills anyway?"

"Oh, just something I used to take ... they're for depression I think ...will make you relax and ... enjoy life again!"

Eventually this innocuous habit grew to control her existence. Drugs began to dominate her life. Taking them made her pain quickly disappear. However the pains and heartache always returned with greater intensity causing her to increase dosages steadily over time. Her need for money increased as well as her drug habit grew and she spiraled into a see-saw existence, feeling high and euphoric for a while and then finding herself living with an overriding despair.

The drug habit forced the need for more money. Stella began 'working' for a woman named Carla, who kept a stable of women and a little black book listing her 'clients,' each of who were known only by code names. The clients paid Carla in advance and she in turn paid her 'girls' by the 'dates' they went on with the clients. It was during an evening during spring when Stella was given her assignment, a man named 'Victor.' Carla wrote his address on a piece of paper that she gave Stella who took a cab to the nice part of the city where even the air smelled of wealth. After leaving the cab she went to the door of an impressive looking apartment and rang the bell. The door was opened by 'Victor.' He stood speechless for a moment as did Stella.

"My God, is that you?" asked Martin Sloan

"Oh, God, is that you?" she responded. They both laughed but it wasn't a happy laugh but a laugh tinged with some embarrassment coated with sadness and perhaps regret. Then finally Martin's gathered his wits and managed to speak.

"Come in," he ushered her into a well appointed room with furnishings only the very wealthy could afford.

"Can I get you a drink?"

"Yes, that would be nice."

"The usual?"

"Yes, that'll be fine." He left and she glanced around at Martin's home. He was always noted for excellent taste and that was evident here. He returned and handed her a drink.

They sipped them while trying to avoid looking at each other. Martin was shocked by her sudden appearance in his life for he had forgotten her after they parted years before. She made small talk about the paintings on the walls. All of them were originals by noted artists, some whose work she recognized from visits to museums years before. He thought that she looked quite well. Her occupation had not destroyed her beauty although a few lines were showing around the eyes. As he sat there saying little his mind raced back trying to remember how they had been together and why their marriage failed. He was certain the breakup was her fault, not his. Yet he somehow felt a strange mixture of guilt and pity. An awkward silence followed. Then after a long pause Martin looked at her.

"You know that we can't do this," he said smiling.

"Yes, I know."

"It's not that you . . . it's that I . . ." Martin did not finish the sentence and looked off at a large abstract painting on the far wall of the room to avoid her eyes. They sat opposite each other in the plush living room simply staring past each other. Martin felt obligated to say something to end their meeting.

"That's a Pollock over there . . . and I have some de Kooning's in the other room, but my favorite is the Franz Kline in the bedroom." He should not have mentioned the bedroom, he thought. But Stella was thinking about the painters he spoke of and was familiar with their work. However she said nothing and silence ensued for several moments until finally Martin felt that he had to say something.

"I'm really sorry about things . . . that they didn't work out for you . . . for me . . . between us I mean . . . and I'm sorry about tonight. I am a bit ashamed of myself and I have to tell you that I haven't used Carla's services for several weeks now . . . trying to mend my ways so to speak. I'm even going to my college reunion tomorrow. Going to visit my old campus, maybe see some old friends, argue politics and religion!" He didn't know why he was saying these things but something in him had softened after seeing Stella. She didn't look much older and something about her was still sweet. He rose and left the room for a few minutes and then returned.

"I've called a cab for you, Stella. It'll take you home."

"Thanks, Martin."

They sat quietly until the cab arrived. Martin escorted her to the curb, a chivalrous act he thought. He paid the driver, and then slipped a wad of bills into Stella's hand. She thought of refusing it but knew Martin was not to be denied anything when it came to money, not the taking and not the giving. Although he had paid Carla already, Martin felt he owed Stella something.

He was sure the evening had devastated her. Had he really loved her once? Why did it disappear? What happened to them? These questions puzzled Martin. He thought of kissing her just before she stepped into the cab. Stella paused for a moment and was struck by the sadness she perceived in Martin's eyes. He on the other hand was unsure of himself, a rare thing for him. Was she waiting for him to kiss her? That thought gradually dissipated as he gently closed the door behind her feeling strangely sad, uncertain if it was for her or for him. He went back inside to pack for his trip to his college reunion.

WYSIWYG

THERE WERE MORE THAN a dozen hikers on the trail, moving   along in single-file over the well-worn trail. Starting at dawn, they walked briskly with only a few paces separating each of them while still in the flat terrain of the valley. After ascending a few hundred feet up the mountain, they slowed to a more reasonable pace. The small parade moved wordlessly, its members following their guide while tasting the pure mountain air. The hikers came from various walks of life but they all shared a common love of nature.

Occasionally the leader stopped and raised his arm. Those following also stopped and stood still looking in the direction that his arm indicated. Only a few yards off the trail to the right could be seen three deer grazing, a mother with two fawns. The hikers stared at them without moving while six large brown eyes stared back at them. Then one by one the deer returned to their feeding satisfied that the onlookers were not hostile. Then the hikers moved several hundred yards until the leader again stopped. He waited until a large snake wiggled across his path. By the time the end of the parade arrived, the reptile had disappeared into the tall grass. The procession then moved up onto a ridge line and came to a large unusual outcropping of rocks. The leader pointed off to the left.

"We are standing atop one of the many geosynclines in the area, which were caused by part of the earth's crust warping downward. If you were standing on that mountain over there a few miles away, you would see the many lines of stratum underlying clearly showing the bending of the earth."

Indeed, to their left only a few yards from the path was a cliff face overlooking a ravine that dropped several hundred feet almost straight down into a valley. Several large rocks sat perched over the promontory looking out beyond it. Two of the hikers sat down on the rocks having decided to rest for a while. They watched the others continue their single file march, descending along the trail for a short distance before disappearing in the wooded area which led up to another rise.

"How far do you suppose you can see from here?" asked one of the rock sitters.

"On a clear day you can see forever . . . at least that's how the song goes."

"Okay, how many miles is 'forever,' smarty?" Smarty sat for a few minutes thinking that over. There was no need to rush an answer. Both of them enjoyed the quiet and the solitude. Silence was for them a golden virtue.

"I reckon if you look beyond the next valley over there you might see about twenty miles or so, give or take."

"But what can you see at that distance?"

"Not much, really, everything gets blurred in the blue haze of the atmosphere. Besides, human eyes aren't all that good at such great distance anyway . . . what did you expect to see anyway?"

"I donno. . .somehow I wanted to see . . . " his voice trailed off as he could not find the words to describe his expectations

". . . there is a part of us that wants to see everything, right?"

"Suppose so."

"Can't do that though, can we?"

"Nope, but we can see lots farther using our imagination and recalling what we have been told by those who do that even better than we do. . .we then might see lots more."

"Infinity? . . . Isn't that the same as eternity?"

"Could be . . . someone once said that eternity and infinity go both forward and backward through time." His companion grunted and they fell silent for a few moments, each mulling over their separate thoughts seeking expression. Finally one of them turned to the other.

"It's mind boggling."

"What?"

"Trying to see the whole thing . . . billions of stars . . . the universe. Once a pictorial map of it came with National Geographic . . . it began with a drawing of our solar system that was compressed along with the sun's neighbors into our galaxy, the Milky Way . . . and that was linked to one of the nearest galaxies . . . the Andromeda . . . which in turn was but a smidgeon in the super cluster that measures some hundred and fifty million light years across." He fell silent again as both of them looked out across the mountains beyond which they could not see.

"God did it . . . he made the whole thing, didn't he?"

"Yup, and we're just a couple of flea-flick spots on one of its smallest spots . . . makes you think doesn't it?" They sat for a few more minutes until one of them decided to hike on and catch up with the others. He bid his companion adieu and followed the trail down the slope and disappeared into the woods beyond. The one who remained closed his eyes trying to imagine the scene that had been described. He began to think out loud.

"It is said that everything can be improved, but there are limits . . . time is one of them . . . and had I begun writing seriously when I was younger . . . who knows? My work might have meant something . . . as it is . . . it is ..." and then he dozed off. It was dark when he opened his eyes later. It was night and it seemed that every star in the sky was waiting as he stepped to the edge of the cliff and peered out at the universe as thoughts ran through his mind . . . it sure is vast . . . almost beyond comprehension . . . millions of galaxies filling space with brilliance resulting from tensions of intergalactic forces in an endless array of time and space. It was like peering into eternity.

He felt himself falling. But not down into the ravine. He seemed to float in some timeless fashion and all the while he enjoyed the splendor of the night sky. It seemed to him that he was at one with the universe somehow. Several minutes passed, he was certain of that, and then he came upon on an unusual scene. He was in some kind of temple or church where a preacher up front was speaking and yet no sound came from his lips.

A choir stood in a semi-circle above the preacher singing softly... familiar words seemingly out of place. . . 'Row, row, row your boat. . .' and it was astonishing to see an open coffin appear in front of them. . . 'Gently down the stream. . .' they continued while the hiker looked on absolutely fascinated by what he was seeing all the while feeling a tremendous sense of tranquility. But suddenly he found himself lying in that coffin staring straight up into the air. Oddly enough he lay there without fear or sorrow. Then looking straight up toward the ceiling, he saw it and the roof above it gradually melt away revealing a powerful light that poured down into his face, almost blinding him.

The hiker woke up with rays of the noonday sun beaming down on him. At first he was puzzled by it all. It took him some time to gather his wits about him. A faint smile moved across his face as he looked down at the trail below and saw the hikers coming back. Soon he would join them and return to the valley where their lunch awaited them.

Xenophobia

His RANCH WAS JUST a few miles from the river. A few hundred yards to the north of the river where he was watching for them, a dirt road ran parallel to the west. Next to that was a large area of desert-like land, harsh and foreboding. Beyond that lay thousands of acres of grazing land that accommodated large herds of beef cattle. They were his. The land was his. Everything was his. In his sense of possessiveness, everything included land bordering his ranch and the great river itself. By God, it's mine!

But the herds were smaller now. Everything was going to hell in a hand-basket. He yearned for the good old days and often thought of them. Long ago his daddy fought the Indians. And he fought those from across the river who once owned this land over here, or at least they lived on it. Shucks, they weren't doing anything good with the land back then, just squatting on it like vultures.

Yes, that's how it was back then. His grand-daddy fought in the war against those Yankees up north and at one time owned hundreds of those other black skinned people who worked for him. But there was more to it. He and others like him shared a strong dislike bordering on hatred for those that were different, those that looked different, or acted different, like those who often crossed that river and entered their land. There was something in the pit of the soul of men like him that made them want to control and dominate others, even if the others were not any threat to them.

Gradually their desires grew into an obsession. It was rooted in a tradition that ran through his blood and through every cell of his body. His father inculcated it in him with stories about his 'grand-pappy' who fought with Jefferson Davis. Them damned Yankees destroyed our way of life was the way he put it. The family plantation was confiscated. The cotton business died away, his great-grandfather moved west and slowly and diligently created the successful cattle raising business which his grandson now ruled over with an iron hand and an iron heart.

Other ranchers who saw their world in the same way often met at a restaurant in town where they talked in hushed tones while sipping coffee, conspiring ways to prevent entry of those trying to cross that river into their country. After all, those foreigners were dark skinned and spoke what to them was yet another ape-like language. In the rancher's eyes 'they' weren't human. God knows, there were enough of them here already. We don't need no more.

Most of 'them' worked at servile jobs. That's all 'they're good for really. He had even hired a few himself. 'They' shoveled manure at one of his barns and did other menial or hard labor tasks, pick and shovel work. But you always had to have someone watch them or else they'd loaf away the time or steal you blind.

And there was the waitress serving their coffee. She was one of 'them.' But that was okay. They could be servants. Long as 'they' mind their own business . . . keep their noses clean. That's all fine and dandy. But hell, they still ain't like us! They'll never be like us! It never occurred to the ranchers that most of 'those' people had been here for generations; many had roots going back to when this land was theirs before the white man took it away from them. Manifest Destiny was ordained by God.

That was for sure. The ranchers and most of the other 'white' folks hereabouts saw it that way, too. By God we'll keep it that way. They wanted it to stay that way at all costs. That was the maxim of those who commandeered the land years ago, conquered 'them' good! Now it was up to the ranchers to keep those intruders out. Something had to be done about it because the goddamned government seemed powerless or unwilling to stop the flood of 'them' despite the protests ranchers often voiced to their politicians.

"Goddamned spics! They keep comin' no matter what the border patrols do or say! Them border patrol guys is just a bunch of useless assholes, that's for sure, piss-ants that's all!"

"What border patrol? I ain't seen hide nor hair of any of them uniformed assholes we pay all our goddamned taxes for. They just ride around in their pickups all day doin' nothin'. Where the hell are they?"

"Never mind them, we'll do it our way."

"Hell yes, we'll take care of 'em!

The ranchers decided that they had to take matters into their own hands. After all, the local sheriff was on their side. They got him elected and he better by God let them do it their way! The ranchers organized their own 'patrol.' Their plan initially was simply to frighten the wetbacks away and discourage them from crossing the river. The ranchers took turns watching the river at various points such as the one where the rancher now stood. It was favored by 'them' because it was one of the narrowest spots along the river.

Usually firing a few shots over the heads of the intruders was enough to send them scurrying back into the skimpy brush along the river. Those that made it over always kept going once they crossed the river. They did little damage to the grazing areas except stopping occasionally to piss or take a shit. The idea of them doing even that on his land infuriated him. It irritated other ranchers as well for they considered their land to be sacred despite the cattle droppings noticeable by eye and nose everywhere.

After crossing through the area, the wetbacks always headed towards the crop lands to pick for whatever measly pay they could get, or they headed further north inland to work in slaughter houses. Every occupation they were able to find was both miserable and dangerous, but they were desperate men willing to do anything to make money.

Now this was his night to patrol a two mile stretch along the river. Guard duty he called it, just like in the Army where he had served with distinction and earned battle stars and several campaign ribbons. Army service confirmed and strengthened his dislike for people that were not like him. He disdained the few Yankees that were in his unit overseas, even those who displayed the valor and courage he so prized After parking his pick-up truck off the dirt road, he strode through the brush and followed a path to a point overlooking the river.

After walking back and forth along the path for a while, he perched as he usually did atop a large boulder. From there he had a commanding view of the area where them bastards would likely try to swim across. He sat quietly smoking, cupping his hand over his cigarette so that its glare would not be seen by anyone over there. He had done this many times, waiting in the dark, then firing his rifle over the heads of wetbacks. That had always been enough.

This past year a few of his shots had hit some of 'them.' Initially it bothered him somewhat to have possibly killed a man, but he had done that all through France and far into Germany so what's the big deal, huh? Same here, right? After thinking it over he realized that 'they' were just like those Germans he killed. Not really men at all. Savages. Like redskins. He felt no remorse or guilt. Why should he? He was master of his land. He relished his power. The idea of life and death appealed to a deep part of his nature. Still, he didn't always shoot to kill, just when the mood struck him. It often did.

Back at his ranch, he was a different person, one that you would not recognize if you had first seen him perched atop that boulder shooting at people swimming across that river. At home he was relaxed and pleasant. His grin ran from ear to ear as he played with his grandchildren.

"Amy, darlin' come sit on your ole granpappy's lap! Tell me what you done at school. And you Bobby Joe, run get me my slippers will ya, hun? Helen did you get that big box of cookies I asked for you to get me . . . these kids is hungry!" He easily slipped into the role of being just another doting grandparent, full of love and attention to their every need and wish.

He never considered that some of 'them' may have grandchildren, or that some of 'them' were not much more than children. Sitting on the rock his weathered face with the piercing eyes peered intently from under a ten-gallon hat. He squinted in the dim light. It had transformed him into something different from what it had been a few hours before. Had he really known himself he might have altered his life and the lives of the group of men who formed the line of shadows approaching the river on the other side.

When he heard the men enter the water, the rancher snuffed out his cigarette, unaware of the twisted look creeping over his face. He waited quietly as the men slowly waded into the water. They were following a large man. They wore only underwear and held their clothing in plastic bags over their heads. Slowly they advanced into deeper water and the leader began to swim.

"Goddammit, here they come!" he thought, "Them bastards got it comin'. . . I'll show 'em!" He waited until the man leading reached the middle of the river. He put the rifle to his shoulder and squeezed the trigger three times. Gunshots echoed across the water, up and down the river banks. All three bullets hit their mark striking the leader. His body stopped moving and partially sank before starting to float downstream. The other men quickly went back and ran frightened hiding in the brush. The rancher lighted another cigarette and he walked nonchalantly back to his truck and drove away.

Yogi

Nicholas Yoganovitch wore eyeglasses throughout most of his childhood. He began wearing them in third grade when it was discovered that his poor grades were due to his poor eyesight. He endured difficulties not only with his school work, but also in any social life he might have enjoyed as a boy. Others made fun of him, calling him four-eyes and other unkind things. They also mockingly called to him using the name derived from Nicholas because it sounded funny. Nicholas did too, and laughed along with them ignoring their taunts until they grudgingly accepted him. Eventually his schoolwork improved greatly and he received very good marks. Then classmates ridiculed him because of his intelligence. No matter, he thought, someday I'm going to be a doctor.

Amazingly, his vision improved to the point where he no longer had to wear eyeglasses and thereafter he wore contact lenses. It was a miracle his mother said, and Nicholas believed that also. Religion was an important part of their family life. His parents were devoted and devout, and his faith supported him throughout life, especially during his service with the Army in Vietnam.

Communism had to be stopped somewhere and Southeast Asia was as good a place as any, Nicholas thought. When the war began he had completed three years of pre-med and after being drafted he was assigned as a medical technician. 'Medics' like him were sent out into the field along with strike forces on 'seek and destroy' missions to repel 'Charlie,' the Vietcong communist soldiers infiltrating throughout South Vietnam.

His greatest fear was showing fear, a trait he shared with many others. Nicholas quickly learned like the others to hide their fear behind wise-cracks and the barracks language common to soldiers. War was never a pleasant thing for those engaged in it and the conditions his unit faced daily were almost unbearable and only grew worse over time. But camaraderie of infantrymen was infectious, prompting young men to perform courageously even as they witnessed the increasing toll of dead and wounded fellow soldiers. The smell of death hung in the air along with the stench of their sweating bodies as they moved through the jungle-like landscape surrounding them.

His unit often found itself in dangerous situations. Nicholas's job as a medic was to care for wounded soldiers. That happened with frequency because his platoon was regularly transported and dropped into free-fire zones by helicopters. He grew extremely proficient at binding wounds. But never became accustomed to seeing torn and lacerated bodies of comrades. Often the enemy was invisible until a fire-fight became full-blown, and then Nicholas usually squinted and wanted to run for cover when bullets began flying. An unknown force kept him from doing so and he stayed in the thick of action until they returned to the base. Even then Nicolas remained with the wounded until they were loading up to be taken to field hospitals, offering encouragement and solace. That was the least he could do.

Out in the free-fire zones, he and other medics moved right along with the infantrymen ready to bind wounds and prepare them for evacuation instead of waiting for bodies bleeding from bullet or shrapnel wounds to be brought to them. Mortal combat saturated the pores of every participant with a persistent feeling of horror that never left. Nicholas occasionally found himself watching fire-fights with awe and several times he ran fearlessly out into the line of fire to reach a fallen soldier.

The pungent odor of cordite mingled with the smell of blood, intestines, severed body parts, and internal organs secreting various solids and fluids along with the life they once held. He learned to quickly stem the flow of blood while observing exposed muscles, bones, and organs. He saw tracers rip through the jungle ahead. He saw his comrades falling. All too often. But if he and the other medics acted quickly, many of the wounded would survive to fight another day. They raced from body to body of men slumped on the ground, binding wounds hurriedly, stopping the flow of blood and injecting pain killers as battle raged around them. Nicholas discovered that while his attention was on the wounded his fear disappeared, or at least was greatly diminished.

He was sometimes called 'Doc' by the soldiers, or 'Yogi,' a name he grew to like. Few even knew his name was Nicholas and that his parents called him Kolya. Usually his unit was delivered to some isolated 'Drop Zone' miles from their base. The target was selected for them by a group of unseen officers planning sorties from unknown locations somewhere far to the rear. Occasionally after being deposited in one of these jungle clearings they sometimes were greeted by an eerie silence. The eyes of everyone around grew wide searching for the enemy in the brush around them. When nothing was seen, they relaxed a bit only to have the silence broken with the deadly rattle of machine gun fire that seemed to come from every direction.

The enemy was stealthy, usually hidden by lush growth of vegetation. Sometimes they lurked in the thatched huts of small villages. The soldiers would drive them and any occupants away and torch the entire village. Yogi often closed his eyes as the helicopter taking him to the 'front' lifted off the ground. He too was a likely target for those bullets that often came from out of nowhere. Actually there was no 'front' like the kind common to previous wars. The enemy appeared and disappeared like ghosts and often a fire-fight ended as abruptly as it had started.

Like other 'medics,' Yogi did not wear the large Red Cross painted on a white circle on his helmet. That only provided an inviting target for enemy snipers. Others around Yogi usually sensed his presence and felt reassured knowing that he was on the mission with them. Yogi exuded an aura of confidence to everyone while keeping his fears hidden and in check. Soldiers in his unit respected him and all the other medics. There would have been a troop rebellion if the medics weren't sent along with them on these forays.

Nicholas had patched up dozens of wounds. He pulled shut the eyes of several who would never again see the light of day. His fear was tempered to some degree by smoking marijuana with others back at their base. Some relied on stronger drugs to dampen their combat traumas. The brutality of war and their miserable conditions required the need to dull the jagged edge of their dangerous existence. Booze was not always available to them and drugs were in prevalent use. As to who would 'get it' on any given mission, it was all a matter of luck he thought. There was no way around that. Fate and fortune mingled on every mission and every patrol. Someone said that there were no atheists during wars, and while his faith sustained him he was surprised to learn of those in his unit who no longer believed in God. Those doubters felt that any God who permitted such insane violence and brutality was not worth worshipping. He watched as some soldiers became beast-like in their strange lust for violence, allowing them to kill indiscriminately without remorse.

"Listen up, men!" their sergeant yelled as the platoon assembled for briefing on the upcoming mission. The soldiers looked sullen and dispirited as a young lieutenant stepped forward to outline the plan for their next adventure and issued some instructions, "You guys just got to move quicker upon leaving the choppers! Hanging around them keeps you and them as inviting targets for Charlie, and you are apt to get your asses shot and our choppers damaged!"

"Fuck the choppers!" someone murmured in back while everyone checked their gear.

"Any questions?" There were none.

Nicholas looked around at the faces of the men about to enter combat again, some for the umpteenth time. He had done this so many times that he had forgotten how many. The faces around him reflected many things, many moods. The pupils of some eyes darted back and forth nervously. Others simply stared dead ahead displaying little emotion and whatever fear they held inside them. Nicholas saw death in the eyes of some, the blank stare of someone half-heartedly resigned to fate. He wondered if any or all of them had that sickening feeling in their stomachs that he usually felt just before boarding the helicopters. Yes, they must have felt that. He did every time. They moved to the staging area where the row of helicopters waited.

Hurriedly the platoon boarded as the blades above them began to whirl. Occasionally all four platoons of the company went on a mission together. Once the whole battalion flew away in a major assault on a remote village that intelligence said was an enemy haven. The olive drab painted machines roared up and away as rotors swatted away at the air above them. The rush of air felt cool compared to the heat on the ground. After reaching the drop zone the huge 'birds' descended to disgorge their cargoes. Soldiers jumped off and quickly hustled to take positions and await action. No damned lieutenant had to tell them to do it quickly. They knew what they had to do. And how.

When the bullets hit him he was unaware of them and continued ministering to the three soldiers lying on the ground near him, moving from one to another trying to calm the fears of those crying out for help. Then someone was yelling

"Get your ass down, Yogi!"

"What the hell you yelling about, Tony?"

"For Christ's sake, Yogi! . . . don't you know you're hit!"

"What the hell you talking about?" Yogi looked down at his right leg. A red river flowed down to his ankle, his leg now covered with blood. It was his blood. He was surprised at how little it bothered him and how calm he was despite the dull pain that he now felt. Yogi expected to get hit sooner or later but now seemed detached watching his life ebbing away. He reached down and applied pressure to his wound to stop the bleeding but just then another medic came to his aid.

"Gotta get your ass outta here, man! But Yogi was still reaching over to patch up yet another wounded man nearby while trying to forget his own wound. Maybe it was just a fucking dream. It was surreal. The chaos around him faded a bit as he began to slip into unconsciousness. In the distance the choppers could be heard approaching. The wounded were hurriedly carried or dragged to the drop zone. Yogi was supported by a soldier on each side and they shoved him aboard one of the choppers with difficulty. One of Yogi's contact lenses fell out and it was strange for him seeing anything now. Things got blurred. The whole fucking world was out of whack. He felt the urge to laugh but coughed blood instead when he tried. As the chopper lifted off, he was no longer conscious. Someone held onto him so he wouldn't fall through the open door.

Yogi spent a few weeks in the hospital before being sent home. His leg would never be the same but he was lucky to be alive he reasoned. Some guys lost legs and arms and others went home in body bags, something he once envisioned for himself. On the trip back to the States he thought about his experiences. Despite the dire warnings about the advance of Communism because of the Domino Theory, it was obvious that the Vietnamese could never attack our country. It was a poor nation. And yet its people fought with grim determination to survive the great firepower of our Army. Anyway, Yogi was done with it forever. He talked with other soldiers who complained bitterly that they should have been allowed to win the war and had been prevented from doing so by the politicians.

"What the hell was there to win?" Yogi asked angrily, "You guys are totally full of shit! There wasn't a goddamned thing worth winning over in that country! Not a dammed thing! The Air Force bombed the shit out of everything they could! But Charlie still kept on coming! After all, it was their country, not ours! You would expect them to fight for it, after all, they kicked the hell out of the French." His anger eventually subsided and he resumed his studies at the university as if nothing unusual had happened.

Eventually Yogi married and he and his wife Lynnette would have three children, two boys and a girl. They would live in a nice suburb not far from the city and the university from which Yogi had graduated with honors. He became a research scientist and thoughts of war were like bad dreams fading from his memory. He concentrated on embryonic stem-cell research and looked forward to significant discoveries that could save lives in a different battle. He had ample reason. His widowed foster mother Freda suffered from Alzheimer's and was confined at a place called Shady Green Acres. Yogi visited her three or four times every week watching her steady deterioration, amazed on those visits when her memory somehow returned for a few precious moments after having been hidden away somewhere in those gloomy shadows of her mind.

"How are you, Kolya?" then after a long pause during which she looked around, "Where am I?"

"Don't worry, mother, they take good care of you here."

"Why don't you come to see me more often, Nicholas?"

"I was here only yesterday, mother."

"Oh, yes . . . yes you were . . . I've forgotten. Did you take your father to church last Sunday like I asked you to? And did you feed Muchka today?" Her husband had died several years before, and Muchka their cat, had been euthanized three years ago after suffering detached retinas. Freda became a resident of Shady Green Acres soon after that. Yogi was pleased that she was vocal this visit. During most visits she was barely coherent.

She would sit immobile staring off into the distance ignoring the flashes of the television set blaring away in the corner. Yogi felt a stab of pain inside as he looked on helplessly during those times. That happened more often than those lucid moments. Yogi worked diligently at the lab, putting in extra hours in a titanic struggle to wrest answers from the contents of test tubes, vials, and the reams of data that had been accumulated over time. He also taught anatomy to a class of pre-med students at the university.

He didn't need the money, but he enjoyed teaching. There was an unexplainable connection he felt with his students. They called him 'Mr. Yogi' after he shared some of his experiences in Vietnam. Later during a pleasant autumn day he visited his mother, but she was unable to communicate. Yogi returned to teach the class at the university and found that a cadaver became available for his class to dissect. They would study the various parts of the human body. They gathered around him. Yogi looked at the form under the sheet.

"This was a human life not long ago . . . treat it with respect for it once lived . . . it is now giving you an opportunity to peer into a human body . . . some say that the body is the temple of the soul, but no matter what you believe, treat it with some reverence." He was pondering over the mysteries of life while he pulled the sheet away slowly, folding it neatly against his body before turning his gaze back at the inert form on the table. It was then that he realized that the body had belonged to one of the men he had often seen playing checkers regularly in the lounge at Shady Green Acres.

Zackary

It WAS A SILENT invasion. No shots were fired. Armies did not clash. The invaders moved quietly and were not detected upon their arrival, having found Earth by detecting and following vibrations emanating from its sun, which was known to them as Astro Helios. The leader of the visitors was called Nageekcaz and although the invaders he led were peaceful, he oversaw their activities with the precision of an astute field marshal.

All of the visitors had remarkable powers. Each of them employed a form of physical and psychic plasticity permitting them to travel through long distances in space and to assume any shape or appearance desired. Each of them now possessed personas blending easily into every society and culture without detection.

The invaders used impressive credentials which they meticulously forged shortly after their arrival.

These visitors possessed telepathic powers to an extremely high degree. Transmission of data was done by applying a form of intense concentration while simultaneously focusing on information to be conveyed and visualizing the recipient. Datum then moved rapidly with precision. The limit of such communications was generally limited to a few thousand miles on any planetary body while in outer space the range was vastly increased.

Three lieutenants led the activities of special teams that possessed more sublime powers. The first group could move back through time. Another smaller group had the faculty to move forward toward eternity. If either team ventured beyond the vortex of ruling forces they would eventually return at the other end of the time spectrum when the past and the future would be one. Then to return to the present required a great deal of time and effort. The third group remained in the present and researched various archives and observed human activities at various points around the globe.

"It is agreed that Elyodmot will accompany those who will journey into Earth's past," said Nageekcaz. He was not an authoritarian leader, and instead all the invaders worked together with unbounded cooperation without rancor or argument. Self-interest was intertwined with the common interest for that was how things were done at planet Veraciapan from which they originated in the galaxy containing Astro Solentia. Those resisting cooperation of multiple thought, action, and feeling succumbed to a law called 'Create or Cease to Exist.' It was because of such cooperative attitudes and manners that the invaders were able to follow emanations of Astro Helios and reach Earth and it solar system.

"And I will accompany those journeying into Earth's future," said Sirrubnoj, "so I assume that Eseilgup will remain in the present, but then Eseilgup has had more experience and has a larger group to coordinate."

"That is so," said Eseilgup, "But if either of you wish I will gladly exchange assignments."

"How far shall we examine the past?"

"Only to the establishment of the planet before moving forward to critical eras where differentiations can be noticed of major progressions and major perturbations."

"And the team moving forward, does it have some limit?"

"The last team going forward at planet Daomikl became disoriented after passing through multiple millenniums, so it is advisable to monitor the team's condition carefully and chose the appropriate turn-back point, but only after sufficient information had been obtained."

No other ideas or thoughts were expressed, and each group deployed to their task of observing and studying all aspects of life past, present and future. Nageekcaz assumed the name, persona, and characteristics of a human called Zackary Keegan. For a time he was employed teaching school, a perfect cover for him. It allowed him access to the educational system of one the major nations on Earth.

Zackary remained at one location awaiting reports that team members transmitted to him. Of course the present team was able to report first. Zackary collated information as it arrived, which were quickly then sent on by special messenger back to the guiding council at planet Veraciapan. Early reports outlined Earth's physical attributes:

topography, geography, temperatures, and barometric pressures at multiple locations along with observable salient geophysical properties. Other reports provided analysis of societal structures of the diverse cultures observed.

"Inhabitants are divided territorially by invisible borders established by custom or force. Others boundaries are formed by nature's rivers, oceans, and mountains. Besides geographically, inhabitants are separated by language, custom, race, economics, ethnicity, religion, gender, language, and something inhabitants refer to as politics. Each contributes to local homogeny but stability varies depending upon multiple circumstances.

"Great cities have majestic structures that dominate skylines in many nations. Smaller cities and villages, well organized, are scattered throughout the lands, and are also quite wonderful in appearance and function. Useful accomplishments and inferred progress made over several millenniums are obvious. Invention of machine and electronic devices facilitate utility, production of products and thus the comfort of most inhabitants.

"Architecture triumphed with audacious use of stone, metal, and glass. Museums are filled with thought provoking images formed by paintings and sculpture. Libraries brim with vast collections of literature defining the mankind's march through time by recording a high level of cogitation illuminating and explaining the possibilities of life. Educational opportunity is widely available while literacy has diminished except in remote areas. Manufacturing and commerce thrive, spurred on despite inefficient methods of transportation and communication. All in all, life on this planet should be seen as a great experience and compares favorably with other planets in other galaxies.

"Control of inhibitions mitigates anti-social behavior and is promulgated by laws created by governments supplemented by religious edict. Order is observed and maintained with observable continuity. Inhabitants remaining intractable are incarcerated for long periods of time permitting tranquility to prevail. Eccentric characteristics, while frowned upon by society, are tolerated when presented as entertainment. Yet many of the most useful discoveries were made by those marching to 'a different drummer' to use their phraseology."

The glowing and more positive aspects of Earth culture were reported to the origin, but later more somber and somewhat disturbing reports arrived. Misuse of energies both physical and psychic created tensions leading to altercations. Resulting conflicts roiled beneath societal tranquility. Misunderstandings and misinterpretations developed, partly because most of them are unaware of multiple levels of learning and are able to function on only one or two. Attention span is minimal and their thought level stagnates on tangibles, the concrete and seldom reaches the understanding of intangibles. Ironically their imaginations carry them into illusion and superstition.

Thus smaller altercations accelerate, belligerent feelings are coagulated within the beings of large segments of societies, distorting a possibility of grasping reality. Disparate views and anger grow disproportionately. Violence resulted. Governments and other organizations manipulate information to further their objectives. Such machinations exacerbate fears. Attitudes and beliefs clash. Small wars quickly balloon into larger ones, and like some strange disease spreads rapidly over civilization.

"The number of violent perturbations involving inhabitants of Earth is astounding," reported teams from many countries, "Most startling is the fact that humans fail to understand and often function irrationally. Records indicate wars are increasingly more common. Political, economic, and religious reasons become justifications for destruction of life and property.

"Technology improved the comfort level of many in advanced areas while large numbers in other areas suffered cruel and abject poverty. Despite production abilities and abundant natural resources, the basic needs of many are not provided for because a practical and equitable method of distribution has yet to be devised. Resulting inequity is but one cause of friction and conflict. At the psychic core of many resides an ingrained desire to control others or gain advantage over them. These characteristics along with incipient greed and corruption appear to be prevalent to some degree within many inhabitants resulting in mistrust of others.

"Crises are created by leaders seeking enemies to punish while pandering to provincial constituents with promises of vengeance, domination, and destruction of enemies. Such attitudes and demeanors are absent in many other parts of the Universe and are diametrically opposed to what is observable at Sigma Pretorius for example." Zackary had visited several planets where cooperation and education are valued as profitable, desirable, and shared. Earth resources are often wasted on warfare instead of creating well-being.

"Wars are extremely costly to the youth. They are placed into horrific situations where some react by committing barbaric acts in order to survive or fulfill vengeful feelings. But mental scars linger in them for whatever life remains. Non-combatants suffer greatly by their proximity to the violence unleashed by military adventures. Efficiency of warfare increased as weapons of greater destructive powers were developed during their twentieth century."

Meanwhile the team going back through time arrived at the formation of Astro Helios where they observed large segments of igneous matter breaking away from it and hurling into space. Molten globs orbiting Astro Helios eventually cooled and the third globular possessed essential elements including carbon bonding agents permitting life forms to emerge.

"Early cellular life drifted in the waters encompassing much of the globe. After several millenniums land creatures formed, some growing to enormous size before yielding to natural perturbations causing their extinction. A quiet period ensued during which other beasts appeared along with creatures that began moving about in an erect manner. Those grew aware of themselves, of each other, and of their differences from creatures preying on them. Fear of beasts and the sometimes un-hospitable environment forced them to band together for survival.

"Consciousness dawned. A primitive form of cooperation developed but a great deal of time passed before the creatures found ways of communicating beyond pointing and grunting. Sounds and gestures transformed into language. Many fought among themselves, killing for possession of territory or mates. Necessity led to curiosity. Imagination grew. The creatures sought help to fight enemies and their mystery and awe of the Universe led to emerging overwhelming emotions. They perceived the sun, moon, and stars. Those along with the beasts around them appeared to have great powers residing in them.

"A disembodied intelligence was perceived. Their fear led to the worship of those powers and led them to deify them: the strange objects in the sky and the beasts preying on them. Thus gods were created, and personalized into images known by them and reflecting them. These matured into beliefs born from their superstitious nature and the beliefs themselves developed great powers that have endured to the present. Before writing and reading were known, oral history was transmitted by older creatures that were revered since they possessed longer life. They told stories which grew into legend and myth that became entrenched in developing minds."

Zackary Keegan studied the report carefully but he had gone with other teams exploring various parts of the Universe, witnessing similar developments on other occasions. But in some cases it took a different turn where life forms controlled and minimized the aberrant behavior and thinking observed on Earth. He listened eagerly to the forward group report, the team that journeyed toward eternity.

"Generally the inhabitants of Earth remained unaware of their slavery to material objects for several centuries. Consumer habits blinded them to understand the realities of life. Between tendencies to destroy other beings of their own species as well as the life of other species, it seemed unlikely that reality will be embraced by them soon.

"They ignored the affects of their habits for many years until some were almost beyond correction. Pollution of earth's atmosphere affected life and as conditions worsened, affected their solar system. After several hundred years of genetic engineering, science redefined life. The inhabitants will evolve physically to adapt to altered environmental conditions and races gradually will merge into one. But Earth creatures did not evolve psychologically as had been observed on other planets.

"They still shun reality much like the inhabitants of the current era, often looking to escape through observing and identifying through popular entertainments and escapist literature. More radical inhabitants alter their sensory perception by chemical means. The former merely destroy their capacity to think, the latter destroy their physical bodies. Leisure time grew but was often squandered in repetitive acts of folly. Those with aesthetic natures desired to live outside of themselves, and discovered ancient ways of accomplishing such states in a manner that did not harm or affect others.

"Great advancement in medical science prolonged life for many but extra time was often lost in drug filled haze. The brain was explored in detail, finding various electrical circuits that were mapped to determine which parts respond to certain medications or stimulus. Unfortunately the individual psyches failed to develop further while sciences forged ahead and although large numbers of inhabitants lived longer, they still produced unnecessary tensions and conflicts with others and within themselves.

"Their habit of saying that which is not so became ingrained and their egos would not relinquish the desire to dominate while there was a false assumption of understanding, one that was not totally true. Suppressing or vilifying others, those differing from them in some respect, was common and there was heavy use of equivocation to create false impressions. Several generations passed before prejudices modified for racism to diminish and then very reluctantly. After our team returned many of them required treatment for depression and anxiety. The observations had created a toxic view of existence never observed before.

"Wars continued on a larger scale well into another millennium beyond which the team decided not to go. More importantly few inhabitants learned to accept their fate, or even approach an understanding the meaning of existence except for what they had been inculcated with. Most earthlings possessed inordinate desires for comfort along with a desperate need for material objects."

Zackary received another report explaining to a greater degree the inhabitant's propensity to ignore reality. Psychological studies indicated two kinds of beings on the planet. Although both possessed identical cranial capacity, one type employed most of its brain in varying degrees, the organ containing opposite and complimentary segments. One brain-part favored intellect and experienced life narrowly. It remains perceptibly negative in its approach to everything. Those creatures were ruled unconsciously by long held beliefs, those remaining unchallenged and becoming barriers to understanding.

The other brain-part, less often used, essentially perceives a broad view of life and its experiences. This part is positive in nature, perceiving things unimpeded by the interpretations foisted upon it by its counterpart. This higher level was found only in a very small number of inhabitants. And even in many of them, the negative portion sometimes presided, limiting unknown potentials. Zackary then met and conferred with his lieutenants for an extended period as they gave their views and opinions on what had been learned during this mission.

"The earth inhabitants of Earth will escape from their narrow and rigid beliefs only after the passage of several more millennium. But at least they pose no immediate danger the Universe at this time."

"Misdirected energies are a constant. Earth creatures do not understand that love and energy are synonymous, a form of concatenation, not to be wasted, but applied with discretion. Most have no sense of harmony when it comes to real living."

"It is unbelievable that earth's inhabitants are so unaware of their own history, so much so in fact that errors perpetrated in one generation are often repeated in the next resulting in gross miscalculations."

"The masses are misinformed and misled despite the many prevalent forms by which information is disseminated on a continual basis. There are at times information over-loads. That and the ego blocks reception and understanding. Thus the inhabitants are incomplete, failing to comprehend existing possibilities. They usually react to stimulus without thought, unconscious of their ways.

"They do not trust those with greater learning and knowledge due to a fear of the unknown. And many of the learned creatures have questioned long-held beliefs. Yet the number of non-believers is growing but most fear to voice their feelings for fear of being ostracized. The spirit of learning is squelched. It is a wonder that progress of any kind emerged while such restrictive thinking occurred during formative years of this planet."

"A small group of individuals who understood, or wished to understand, were primarily responsible for material progress, tangible things. It was inventors, poets, and other artists whose work made palpable gains in the direction of living more fully."

"The Earth creatures' knowledge is limited by their apathy toward learning and expanding their understanding."

"Intelligent beings ponder whether fate is determined by circumstances ... events and other people . . . as opposed to personal character, a trait relying more on the self."

"Can they survive with their gods?"

"Can they survive without their gods?"

"Sadly . . . most of them cannot trust themselves."

"They will go on killing each other as well as other species during the foreseeable future, and they will eventually do harm to their own planet before realizing how to know themselves."

"It is clear that the inhabitants are cunning and often ruthless in obtaining their desires . . . and despite that they all derived from beasts it was observed that beasts kill only for food while the inhabitants kill for power and pleasure."

"Yes, many of them seem unaware of . . . even fearful of their potential . . . something that could serve them better if realized and applied to reaching a more cooperative life."

"Yet it is true that a great many of the inhabitants are basically sound . . . well intentioned and usually well-meaning in their thought and feeling despite their tendency to equivocate or say that which is not so."

"But their deep seated desire for vengeance and their being unaware of their violent nature is appalling."

"Still, deception and intrigue have been witnessed by our teams at other places in the Universe as well so that such characteristics can be expected here on Earth as well."

"But there is nothing that can be done for them and their fate is sealed by their own psychic propensities."

A decision was made. The members of Zackary Keegan's teams again made the excruciating effort required to master several stages of being by employing secret forces. Those neutralized inter-planetary gravities and energies that include electro-magnetic and wave forces plus hidden forces of which they were cognizant. The resulting energies they then created were multiplied and condensed permitting them to reformulate, turning their essences into a continuous energy-flow that penetrated and nullified the alternating attraction and repulsion of forces dominating throughout the Universe. They were able to pass through existing multiple galaxies and return to from where they emanated. One by one, just as surreptitiously as they came, all the members of the various teams quietly vanished into the silence from which they had come leaving Earth to its destiny for the time being.

ABOUT THE AUTHOR

ANDREW FRANK KLIMKO came to writing late in life despite an interest in literature and perhaps because of it. As a youth his focus was sports: football, baseball, tennis, bowling and sailboat racing. He served in the Army twice, first in Korea and Japan following World War II and in Germany during the Korean War. A graduate of Miami University at Oxford, Ohio, he was employed by the Postal Service where he held several positions including a brief tenure as a postal inspector. He retired as superintendent of operations. For many years he directed and acted in community theater groups and participated in Great Books discussion programs. He has been involved in the Gurdjieff Work for over twenty years. After his retirement he wrote *And So Forth And So On, Memoirs of an Ordinary Man* before turning to fiction.

Printed in the United States
101445LV00004B/1-27/P